Dordy dropped his hand

"I ought at least to give
you to get mixed up in
you'd behaved like an average citizen – given your
testimony and shown impatience to get on with the fun of
the carnival – you'd probably not have been bothered
again. By doing more than this minimal civic duty,
you've probably marked yourself out as a potential
danger to a lot of very dangerous people."

"But – this sounds like a historical melodrama!" Horn
objected.

"Isn't it dramatic that a man should have been hounded
from planet to planet, driven out of the regions where his
reputation protected him to Earth where his immunity no
longer held good – and killed?"

"That's not just something you worked out from looking
at the booklet you gave me. How do you come to know so
much about this Lars Talibrand?"

"I can only promise you that you could learn exactly the
same facts as I know if you took the trouble to go and look
for them."

"I'm going to," Horn said determinedly.

INTO THE SLAVE
NEBULA

JOHN BRUNNER

CORGI BOOKS
A DIVISION OF TRANSWORLD PUBLISHERS LTD

INTO THE SLAVE NEBULA
A CORGI BOOK 0 552 12012 X

Originally published in Great Britain by Millington Books Ltd.

PRINTING HISTORY

Millington edition published 1980
Corgi edition published 1982

This book is set in 10/11¼ pt 'Monophoto' Old Style

Corgi Books are published by Transworld Publishers Ltd.,
Century House, 61–63 Uxbridge Road, Ealing, London W5 5SA

**Made and printed in United States of America by
Offset Paperbacks, Dallas, Pennsylvania.**

CHAPTER I

IN THOSE last few months Lars Talibrand traveled far and fast—from system to system, from star to star, back-tracking, making false trails whenever he could spare a precious day or two. But he could not elude the patient death that dogged his footsteps.

He went from Vernier to Arthworld to Creew 'n Dith; from Creew 'n Dith to Newholme to Mars. He came at the last to Earth in carnival time, when all the world was making holiday, and there, in a high chamber in a hotel overlooking on the one side a fairground's tumult and on the other a placid inlet of the sea, he met his destiny.

When that was done which certain people had decreed must be done, the news of its doing went the way Lars Talibrand had come. This news traveled faster than he had been able to, even in the knowledge that more than his life depended on speed.

And on worlds scattered across the galaxy certain men, certain women, breathed easier because Lars Talibrand breathed no more.

Blasting bands, chanting choirs, performing animals with expressions of patient tolerance at the foolishness of the antics their human masters forced them to exhibit, hordes of feverish revelers shouting, throwing streamers, laughing as though the whole world was the stage for a vast slapstick comedy—the carnival processions paraded past the hotel in which Lars Talibrand could not hear them.

Why not? After all, tonight and for the week to come, this planet Earth *would* be the stage for a comedy, the farce of carnival in which all could become Pantaloon, Harlequin, Columbine, by turns.

Processions such as these were winding through the streets of every town on the terminator; as the sunset moved around the planet, others would join them.

Now, down by the beach, androids were making the last checks before turning on the colored lights, setting loose the tiny organisms which would make the very ocean glow; the service robots tested each other's circuits, making sure beyond doubt they would not fail during the coming week. In the fairgrounds the concessionaries—all amateurs, those who preferred to enjoy themselves by helping others to do so—were setting up their booths, marquees, stalls, their gyrodromes, switchbacks, grav-free dancehalls. Trucks full of miscellanea lumbered up, bringing the last batches of sweetmeats, novelties, practical joke kits, flasks of wine, masks, dueling swords, aphrodisiacs and a thousand other things.

Householders were taking the last of their valuables to the public repositories to be stored behind time-locked doors until carnival was over. People had been known to lose themselves so completely in the frenzied half-world of the week-long festival that they pledged away everything they owned and woke next Oneday into the dismal universe of the grey-clad Dispossessed, there to mourn away two statutory years as the most miserable of conscious beings, less lucky than robots, less secure than androids. So the prudent, aware of their own fallibility, insured against the possibility.

Owners of family groundcars and helis were likewise time-locking the controls. During carnival no one could possibly want to go anywhere in a hurry, of course—unless, for instance, to hospital after a heart attack. There was no business, no urgent appointments to be kept apart from romantic rendezvous . . . and it was a dedicated lover indeed who could maintain his fidelity in face of hundreds of fresh and willing partners. Along the streets, on the beaches and the lawns of the many parks, robots were distributing the free bubbletaxis, little open two- and four-seater drifters, which could be relied on to take their

6

passengers *somewhere*, but which could not be directed until daybreak. After dawn it was permitted to give them an address—your own, or anyone else's—but until then it was up to random robot selectors to choose their destinations.

The sky above shone a luminescent darkening blue, with hardly a cloud to be seen. It would have to rain, here and there across the face of Earth, some time during carnival week, in order to preserve the meteorological balance of the atmosphere. But it would rain so far as possible out to sea, and at a local time when most of the revelers would be sleeping.

Catering wagons were falling in behind the carnival processions—thousands of them. There had to be thousands. No place of business remained open during carnival save the fairground concessions, and that included food shops and restaurants.

Now, as the sun went down, the luxury stores which had remained open to meet the last-moment demand for wigs, cosmetics, perfumes and fancy dress, began to resonate to the subtle low-frequency sonics that made the clients vaguely uncomfortable and encouraged them to depart from the premises. Much relieved, leaving the problem of working out their accounts for the fantastically profitable few days just past, until their return to work, the human staff hurried to change and join the crowds. A little wistful, their android assistants locked up behind them, taking their time, wondering what could be done with the next seven empty days.

Merriment and rejoicing like a river of wine, a day of sunshine, a breaking wave of light, engulfed the world, and there were few who noticed that—like a temperate summer—it was here and there patched with grey.

Derry Horn drew back from the window overlooking the roadway. The last of the processions had streamed into the fairground, and electric organs were drowning the strains of the parade bands. Time now to dress and go

7

to join the fun.

At a curt command the windows went opaque, matt-surfaced so as not to spoil the carefully planned indirect lighting with accidental reflections. He gave another direction, and closet doors slid back to reveal the selection of costumes he had ordered for carnival. There was something for every possible mood in the range he had chosen—or so he had thought. But now, as he fingered the silks, the stiff parchments, the glitter-weaves, he found himself oddly at a loss.

No: not "oddly." He made the admission with a weary sigh. Rather the phrase should be: "as usual."

Irritated, he seized one of the outfits at random and threw it across the chair. At once he began to wonder what in the world had made him choose *that* one. Once more . . . "as usual"!

Resolving to put the costume on anyway—and the hell with it—he slipped out of his ordinary day-clothes and crossed to the bathroom at the side of his suite to freshen up. When he left the shower he stepped into the drying cabinet adjacent, switched one of its walls to a mirror setting, and regarded himself thoughtfully as gentle warmth sucked the moisture off his body.

This is you, he told himself. *This is Derry Horn at twenty-two.*

He saw a dark-haired young man with pale skin and dark blue eyes. Around his full mouth there was a noticeable slackness, a quarter-way towards being a pout. The flesh of his arms and thighs was unfirm, shaking just a little to his movements. The paleness of his skin and the darkness of his hair combined to make his cheeks and chin almost—not quite—blue, like watered milk, shadowed by roots of beard that not even the most efficient modern depilatory could remove.

He touched his face, wondering what atavistic compulsion still made men think it unmanly not to be able to grow beards even though they spent so much time trying to prevent them showing. Maybe it was just that they had

8

to have something which opposed their will? There certainly wasn't much else in this disciplined world which resisted their whims.

He grew aware that he was thoroughly dried, and left the cabinet. With the removal of his weight from its floor, the soft blasts of hot air ceased their hissing.

On his return, the costume he had laid out looked even more ridiculous. But when he glanced at the still-open closets, he could see nothing that was more to his present taste. Naked, he threw himself down in a padded chair and struck a smokehale. This was a lunatic state to be in, the first night of the carnival!

It crossed his mind that a drink might help, and he called for a waiter, which came swiftly. This hotel where he was staying offered perhaps the best service in the world—and since the world was Earth, that meant the best in the galaxy. Naturally, too, its robots were by Horn & Horn....

Prompt, silent, the waiter emerged from the service aperture and halted before his chair in mute inquiry, its lean plastic body glistening under the lights. For a moment he felt inclined to compare its rather beautiful quasi-human form with his own flabby nudity, but the notion was stillborn; he had been surrounded by robots since he was born, and nothing could make him regard them as more than mechanical conveniences.

"I want something to snap me out of a fit of depression," he said abruptly. "What do you recommend?"

The waiter hesitated. "I'm not programmed to prescribe for illness, sir," it said apologetically. "Might—?"

"I'm not ill!" Horn snapped. "I just want a euphoric of some kind. The best you've got."

"I could get you the most expensive," suggested the waiter diffidently. "I presume that would be the best. Although, to be honest, I've heard from various clients that others in a lower price-bracket were more to their taste...?" It let the words die away, cocking its head.

Oh, for—! Horn fought the temptation to curse aloud. What had possessed his father and grandfather to discontinue the nice uncomplicated robots of his early childhood, which could be relied on to do what you told them without argument, in favor of these "sophisticated" new models that puzzled and prevaricated over the simplest request?

"It'd make things a sight easier if the management put androids on waiter duty instead of robots!" he exclaimed. "At least they'd have some idea of how the stock tastes!"

With a faint air of protest, the waiter said, "If you'll permit me to correct you, sir, it wouldn't help at all. Androids are prohibited from indulging in liquor or any other stimulant, as you doubtless know."

"One could get around that," said Horn, with the certitude of a man who has got around many regulations. He had. He belonged to a wealthy family, even by the standards of a wealthy age. "But all a drink would do to you would be to short your circuits out."

Suddenly the ridiculousness of arguing with a robot struck him, and he began to chuckle. The waiter made a solicitous move forward, and he waved it away.

"You didn't tell me which euphoric you desire," it said.

"Doesn't matter," Horn said, getting to his feet. "Forget it."

"I'm physically unable to forget anything," said the waiter proudly. "In fact it took me a long time to calculate the implications of the concept." Then it was struck by the possibility that such an admission might be taken to reflect on the quality of its parent company's products, hesitated again, assigned the problem—as it had been designed to do—to the category "dilemma," and returned to the service aperture, its plastic feet hushing on the heavy pile of the carpet.

When it had vanished, Horn put on his carnival costume and gave a final glance around the room, his headquarters for the week. Well, that was a change, anyway. Maybe the change would make the difference.

10

Somehow or other he had *got* to enjoy himself! If he didn't reawaken that ability he might lose it forever, and his whole life would monotone down to the same flat round of boredom from which he was trying to escape. Last year's carnival had been so far from the memories of the ones he had enjoyed as a child—or even as an adolescent. They had been marvelous; memory swore that to him. Last year's had been—in a word—dull.

This year, therefore, a different city. A hotel room instead of his family home to come back to when he was worn out. No one related to him within a thousand miles. Maybe it was the cloying circle of his family which had ruined his fun last year.

Maybe.

He hated to think of what his future would be like if it was not his surroundings that were at fault—if the flaw lay in himself. To face a hundred more years of mere existence; never to experience excitement; grey day after grey day . . .

Perhaps he should have had that euphoric after all.

CHAPTER II

HE WENT reflexively to the personal elevator connected to his suite, and had called for it before he remembered: carnival week had officially started now. Instead of the elevator rising in its shaft, a speaker on the wall came to life and with dulcet tones gave him a recorded reminder.

"It's carnival week, sir! In the interests of good fellowship and companionability, the hotel has withdrawn the personal elevator service in favor of the main elevators. Please leave your suite and turn left along the corridor to locate the nearest operating elevator. We hope

11

you meet congenial acquaintances there even before you join the merry throng outside!''

When he was sixteen or seventeen, he and a bunch of student friends had discovered this custom of hotel managements, and had spent half an evening making absolutely certain that hotel residents *did* meet interesting company in the elevators. They had got themselves up to look like decaying corpses—blue-faced, puffy-handed, with wall-white contact lenses on their eye-balls—and laid themselves down on the floors of empty elevators to await results. Their score had included four cases of hysteria and a heart attack. They had thoroughly enjoyed themselves.

Somehow, though, it didn't seem so funny now he looked back on it. He hoped no one here had had the same idea—or at any rate, that no one would put it into practice this early in carnival week.

He had not used the corridor outside his suite since his arrival. Presumably the robots which had brought his baggage had come that way, but he himself had come up in the personal elevator. Anyone booking a suite the size of his was entitled to expect that much privacy. Consequently there was an indefinable deserted air about the corridors, not in any form so perceptible as dust on ledges, or an echo—simply an absence of human passage.

He walked quickly because the sensation his surroundings induced in him was disturbing. He pressed the call button and looked uneasily along both the passages which met at right angles close to the elevator well. A few paces distant in the corridor which he had not taken a pile of baggage belonging to some late arrival was waiting to be put into store; otherwise there was no hint of occupation. He shivered slightly, cursing the compulsoriness of carnival.

Abruptly there was a movement among the stacked empty cases. An arm shot into view, as though thrown out by a man lying on his back. At the same moment he heard a low moan.

12

It might have been a word. It might have been, "Help!"

So someone had had the same idea as he and his student friends. Oh well: it was a standard gag, only funny the first time around. He pressed the call button again, wishing the elevator would hurry.

The arm drew back. A leg was flung wildly into the air and came down on the floor with a slamming noise. The violence of the movement was insane. There was a hint of a crunch mingled with the impact, as though a bone had broken. And a scream.

The agony behind the cry cut through Horn's assumptions. This was no carnival joke! That sound had its roots in pain!

He found himself already moving towards the source of it.

The skin on the back of the hand which showed beside the baggage pile was blue. Android. But nonetheless a feeling being, capable of suffering. Heavy-looking cases were piled over and around his body; others, formerly laid on his legs, had been spilled aside. Inch by inch the victim was drawing back the leg he had kicked out, as though in preparation for another wild spasm.

"Service!" Horn yelled, throwing back his head. The call vanished into the length of the corridor. Then he bent to haul the concealing cases clear. Empty, they were quite light, but he was unused to lifting even light objects— that was a job for robots. He was sweating before he had swept aside half a dozen of them. Only then did he look down at what he had uncovered ... and came close to vomiting.

In the shadow, the android's blue skin looked grey, like a sick human being's. His features, of course, were altogether human. Had been, rather. Someone had beaten him savagely about the head until his eyes burst, his nose was mashed flat on his left cheekbone, and his teeth were broken from their sockets. It was the eyes that were the most revolting.

13

Horn had never felt so helpless in his life. Half of him insisted that he go away, quickly, get to the elevator and so out to the street to join the carnival. The other half of him ached to do something to relieve the pain the mutilated android must be suffering. One ought not to leave even a dog or cat in such dreadful agony, let alone a creature which could stand up and talk to you, whatever the color of its skin. But he did not know how to begin—or whether it was worth beginning.

He was staring sickly around when a voice hailed him from behind.

"Say, friend! Was it you called the elevator before I did?"

He turned his head. A pudgy man of middle age in a parti-colored jester's suit was hailing him from the door of the elevator car. It must have arrived a moment previously.

"Yes! Yes—but . . . look, come here, will you?"

The pudgy man chuckled. He had the indefinable air of a person of great wealth—though if he was spending carnival here on this floor of this hotel, that went without saying.

"*Oh*-oh! At it already, are you? What's behind that stack of baggage—a booby-trap of some sort?" He shrugged. "Well, I'll buy it. It's carnival time, after all."

He trotted from the elevator and came to peer over Horn's shoulder. From the sudden catch in his breathing Horn knew he had canceled his assumption about booby-traps.

"Hey!" the pudgy man said in a low voice. "That's messy, isn't it? Wonder why the garbage robots haven't cleared it up."

"He was hidden under these cases," Horn gestured. "It looks as though he was beaten unconscious, and only recovered enough to push the cases away and call for help just as I came by."

The pudgy man drew back a couple of steps, unable to tear his gaze away from the hideous spectacle, as though at once repelled and fascinated by it. "I should—ah—I should leave it, young fellow." he muttered. "It'll be cleared away soon enough, no doubt."

"But why should anyone want to *do* such a thing?" Horn burst out, clenching and unclenching his fists in frustration as the android gave another sobbing moan.

"You're young," said the pudgy man. "But you're not that young, surely! Looks to *me*"—condensing into the phrase implications of superior maturity and worldliness—"as if some sadist got started on his carnival fun early. Must be rich, too; he'll get a whopping bill for this from the management!" He shuddered. "I hope he confines himself to androids, damn it—wouldn't recommend my worst enemy to help whoever did this to get his kicks!"

"But I can't just leave him lying here!" Horn exploded.

"What else can you do? If you have a dueling sword with you, I guess you can fetch it and put him out of his misery, seeing you're so worried. *I'm* not the dueling type—don't own a sword. Ah, don't fret, young fellow!" He laid a comforting hand on Horn's shoulder. "Service is pretty good in this hotel, you know. They'll get rid of it soon."

A speaker by the elevator announced that there was another call, and unless a passenger entered within thirty seconds the car would go to another floor. The pudgy man muttered, "Excuse me," and hastened back the way he had come.

He just made it before the door shut.

Alone once more, Horn felt tears starting into his eyes as the android, conscious enough to have realized that there were voices nearby, tried to lift his hands and clutch at the world he could no longer see. His mouth had been torn at the corners; he attempted to articulate words, but they were shapeless and muffled with blood.

That blood was as red as any human being's. Overcoming his revulsion, Horn took the blue-skinned hand within his own. The android whimpered like a

15

frightened child and pressed it feebly, drawing at least a shred of comfort from the contact.

Why the hell hadn't robots come running when he shouted for service? He swung around angrily to call again, and was startled to find someone—who had approached unheard—already standing only a few feet away. Beginning with the well-pressed cuffs in front of him, his eyes took in the dark business clothing, not of good quality but neat enough and well cleaned. By this simple fact, that here was somebody still in working garb when everyone human in the city had changed into carnival rig, he knew that at the top he must encounter the blue face of another android.

"It was good of you to do that much for him," the newcomer said in a soft voice. "I'm afraid it doesn't look as though there's much else that can be done—is there?"

"What?" Horn was briefly confused. Nothing in his entire life had so rocked his personality as this encounter with the victim of a sadist's lusts ... if he was to believe the explanation offered by the pudgy man.

"I mean holding his hand like that," the newcomer said. "If you'll excuse me, sir ...?"

Dazed, Horn drew back. With swift economical movements the android dropped on one knee beside his fellow, produced a diadermic syringe as neat and deadly looking as a pistol, and applied it to the upturned veins of his wrist. In a moment the writhing and moaning stopped.

Meanwhile, Horn had risen to his feet, unsteadily. "You—ah—you're on the hotel staff?" he asked. His voice was brusquer than he intended, but otherwise it might have broken.

Wary, as though expecting a complaint about the quality of the service which permitted a guest to encounter such a shocking sight as this, the android nodded.

"I'm the manager's secretary, sir," he said. "For the duration of carnival, of course, that makes me effectively the manager—my chief went to the fairground half an

16

hour ago. On his behalf, I'd like to apologize for this unfortunate incident."

"Unfortunate!" The word burst out at the shrill top of Horn's vocal register. "But this is terrible!" And, catching the android's threatened renewal of apology before it could be spoken, he plunged on. "No, I don't mean my finding the poor devil beaten up and lying here! I mean that anyone should want to do such a horrible thing!"

There was a moment of tense silence, during which the android seemed to be evaluating what he had just heard. At length he said, "It's kind of you to express such concern, sir. But no doubt the perpetrator will be charged for what he has done."

"Is that all you can think of—someone having the cost of his fun added to his bill?"

Once more the android hesitated. Abruptly he relaxed. He said in a tone which bordered on the confidential, "Frankly, sir, *no*. That's the last thing which concerns me. But the—is culprit too strong a word?—the *person responsible* hasn't committed a crime, you know. We may be expensive, but we are replaceable."

"But surely—"

"Oh, certainly my colleague was trained, and valuable to the hotel. He was the floor manager, incidentally. He—"

"*Was?*"

"I gave him a shot of comatine." The android hefted his diadermic, glanced down at it thoughtfully, and returned it to his pocket. "One learns to judge whether an android is damaged beyond hope of economical repair. Latchbolt would need new eyes, and that is usually the break-even point."

"This happens all the time?" Horn was pale with horror.

"I wouldn't say that"—in a judicious tone. "But during carnival one generally reckons to lose two or three of the staff."

Horn stared at the expressionless blue face. His bowels were churning, and the straight lines of the corridor seemed to be twisting at the limits of his field of vision. After a short eternity he managed to say, "But do you know who did it?"

"We may find out. We may not. There's also insurance to cover this kind of risk." The android sounded bored, but under the veneer of calm Horn thought he could detect bitterness, veiled as if by smoke. "And now, sir, if you'll excuse me, I hear the cleaning robots approaching to dispose of Latchbolt's remains."

Ironically he concluded, "No doubt you will be wishing to get out on the street and join in the fun."

Horn shook his head. "No—uh—no! With this fresh in my mind, how the hell do you think I could enjoy carnival? I guess I'll get back to my room and give myself a chance to recover from the shock."

Very conscious of the android's gaze following him, he started along the corridor. He had gone twenty paces before he realized he was heading in the wrong direction. Of course—he had turned a corner by the elevator.

Furious at his own stupidity, embarrassed at being seen to make a mistake by this android whose coolness and composure made him feel like a blundering teenager again, he swung around intending to retrace his steps. As he turned, he caught a quick glimpse through the partly open door of the nearest suite. Beyond that door . . .

Gasping, he strode forward and slammed the door aside. "Here!" he called. "Come here!"

This body was not as ugly as the mutilated android but it reinforced ugliness already in his mind, and his head swam.

Unhurriedly, the android came after him. "What is it, sir?" he inquired.

"Your chance to catch the *culprit* who beat your colleague to death!" Horn stepped across the threshold of the suite. It was identical with the one he himself had been assigned. Except for its occupant.

18

"The chances are the same man did both, aren't they?" he pressed on, having to lick lips suddenly gone hot and dry. "And even in carnival week I guess the lawforce has to take an interest in murder."

He was red-haired, this man, and his skin was a human shade. He lay on his back on the carpet, whose pile had spread out a little under his weight, like grass. His eyes were open and fixed unseeing on the ceiling. A large sharp wooden-handled knife protruded from his chest just over his heart, and—presumably because with his last dying strength he had tried to pull the blade free—his hands were loosely disposed around it, as though folded on his chest by a compassionate hospital attendant.

CHAPTER III

AFTER MUCH DELAY lawforce headquarters furnished a team of investigators: four android technicians under the leadership of a human superintendent named Coolin whose every movement demanded silently why he should have to be on the job while everyone else was out having fun. He struck smokehale after smokehale as his subordinates probed the suite and the adjacent corridor, and chewed the mouthpiece of each into fragments before it had burned down.

A few minutes before their arrival, the comatine shot administered to the dying android had depressed his metabolism to the point of no return. Apparently unconcerned at losing the chance to have the attacker named by the victim, Coolin confined his work to having solidos taken of the dead man and the battered android, and a few curt questions addressed to Horn and the android acting-manager—whose name, Horn had by now established, was Dordy. Earth had for long been so rich that her authorities could afford to be lenient with the citizens, and many of the ancient motives for crime had vanished, for example poverty—no one on the planet was underprivileged bar the Dispossessed who brought their fate upon themselves. Nonetheless, Horn had retained from childhood a romanticized conception of the efficiency of the lawforce, and his first-ever encounter with the casual reality shocked him almost as much as the discovery of Latchbolt's mangled body.

"All right!" Coolin grunted. "Let me just get the whole thing straight. Who was he, anyway?"

Dordy shrugged. "When he arrived he gave the name of Winch. That may not be his own, but during carnival . . ." A delicate gesture with one lean blue hand. "I try always to welcome our clients personally and inquire if they are satisfied with our service. I talked to him yesterday, about noon. I noticed that he spoke with an accent I did not recognize."

Coolin grunted. "But you must have a pretty cosmopolitan crowd in a place like this. Don't you get guests here from all over?"

"All over Earth," Dordy agreed. "Consequently I judged him to be from off the planet."

Lowering himself into a padded chair, Coolin regarded the corpse, encased on the floor within a faintly shimmering stasis field to prevent rigor and putrefaction setting in. "An ordinary knife. And in the chest. Odd, that. Supposing someone wanted him out of the way *that* badly, he could have waited till tonight and provoked a duel with him. If he didn't have the courage he could have slipped him a shot of poison. There are plenty that will addle the brain before a medic can come to the rescue. But he tackled him face to face with a knife. To me that spells the settlement of an off-world score. Hmmm? And so many foreigners come to Earth for carnival, we probably don't stand a snowball's chance on Mercury of catching the man responsible. He'll leave on the first starship after schedules revert to normal next Oneday."

20

His eyes, roaming around the suite, paused on Horn's pale face framed by the back of just such another chair as the one he himself was sitting in.

"Not a coward's way of doing things," he murmured. "Face to face with a knife. Maybe he yelled?"

"That would have attracted the attention of our floor manager, sir," Dordy said. "The waiter robots aren't programmed to respond to random noises, only to clearly spoken commands. Your killer must be a big man, sir— and strong, to have smashed in Latchbolt's face."

"Assuming the same man did both." Coolin tossed aside the latest of his smokehales.

"This corridor!" He gestured through the open door. "People don't use it much?"

"Except for carnival time, people don't use it at all," Dordy agreed, employing the special android use of the term "people."

"So what's it there for?" Coolin countered.

"Android and robot staff, sir," Dordy explained. "Cleaning robots pass along it twice a day and whenever they are sent for, and the floor manager always checks clients' suites during the occupants' absence, to verify the operation of all facilities."

"So until you shut down the personal elevator service, a killer could have come and gone unnoticed except by robots which are too discreet to comment on human behaviour, and one—one, yes?—android who is now dead thanks to your intervention." Coolin's tone was curiously colored with satisfaction; Horn wondered whether it was due to learning that his case looked superficially insoluble and therefore could be left over until after carnival instead of being followed up at once, with all the attendant difficulties.

Dordy, owing to the blue skin, could not pale with fury, but Horn suspected that a man in the same mood would have done. Words seemed to be ground out of his mouth like flour from a mill.

"Administering comatine to Latchbolt was a routine

21

action, *sir!* Had I realized that you would be so severely delayed on the way here, I would have withheld the shot even though it meant his continued suffering!"

"Hoity-toity!" Coolin said, rising. "I'll remember that, blueboy! And I'll make sure it comes to the attention of your chief next week that you were more concerned about the fate of another android than what had happened to a human client of the hotel!"

He rounded on his assistants, standing in a group by the door with their technical equipment festooned around them.

"Record Mr. Horn's testimony, you! And I guess you'd better get something from Dordy as well, though since he's so emotionally wrought up over his blue pal's death I don't know if it'll be worth anything in a court. Shift the bodies directly you finish. I'll be down at the reception lobby checking the registration records."

He marched out.

Recording the testimony took only a short time. Then the dead man and the dead android were carried off in a floater which bobbed up to the windows of the suite— clearly it would not be good for the hotel's image to remove corpses by any route where guests might see them.

And it was over.

Horn remained in the chair where he had sat since Coolin's departure, staring at the spots of blood on the carpet but not remembering the red-haired man who had lain there peacefully—picturing instead the android who had died in agony.

Some people, he was abstractly aware, found violent death the most thrilling thing in the galaxy, able to tickle the most jaded palate. After his first-year brush with reality, Horn realized he was not one of those people. He had found the whole affair sordid and sickening.

The entry door of the suite slid back again, and there was Dordy once more, this time accompanied by two functional cleaning robots. On seeing Horn, he checked in mid-stride.

"I'm sorry, sir! I didn't realize you were still in the room. I was going to have the blood removed from the carpet while it's still wet."

"Tell 'em to go ahead," Horn sighed, but made no move to leave the suite. For a while the only sound was the faint buzzing of the machines cleaning the floor; then suddenly, Dordy spoke up.

"You were wrong, weren't you?"

"About what?" Horn groped.

"About my chance to discover who it was who committed the crimes." Dordy stressed the plural. Ordinarily Horn might have found the android's assumption of person-to-person equality, without the deferential "sir" attached to every remark, irritating. Right now he was too shaken up to care.

"I guess I see what you mean," he muttered. "I wasn't too well impressed by Superintendent Coolin myself. Still, I guess we're just too habitually law-abiding on Earth these days to attract a high caliber of human recruit into the lawforce. The carnival season apart, there can't be very many violent deaths nowadays in the course of a year."

"Two to three murders per million of the population," Dordy said. The robots had withdrawn from the soiled area of carpet, and he stared down to make sure all traces of blood were gone, then scuffed at the pile with his foot. "Not counting android killings. There are a good many of those, but nobody keeps the statistics."

Horn shifted uncomfortably in his chair. A little surprised at his own directness, he heard himself say, "It must be rough to be—to be one of you."

"It is." Dordy's eyes fixed on his face. "Want to know how rough? The insurers who cover me for the hotel management impose a condition of my policy: I mustn't set foot outside the hotel during carnival week unless they pay a surcharge of one thousand per cent on the basic

23

premium. I stop being insured the moment I step over the threshold.''

Unexpectedly, he laughed. "Sorry, Mr. Horn. I'm presuming a hell of a lot on the strength of one decent gesture you made. I apologize.''

Horn got up and walked over to the nearest window. From here he could see down to the shore of the bay, where dark paddleboats were churning up the polychrome luminescence of the sea. Bubbletaxis were drifting on the breeze like balls of thistledown. Very faintly, from the fairground at the other side of the hotel, there came the intermingled tunes of a score of loud-blasting calliopes.

"It didn't seem to me as though Coolin was very eager to go hunting the killer of—what did you say his name was?''

"He said his name was Winch. As I pointed out that may well not have been the truth.''

Horn nodded. "Anyway! Coolin seemed a sight less keen than his androids were to catch up with whoever did for Latchbolt." He made his tone challenging, and Dordy responded with a sarcastic grin.

"Thinking that we don't have families, or relations? That we come out of a chemical vat instead of a womb? That makes us all brothers, Mr. Horn. All of us.''

"I'd like it a lot better if people cared more about each other,'' Horn said, almost inaudibly because he had been brought up to distrust sentimentality.

"I'm afraid you have thousands of years of history opposed to you, sir,'' Dordy said.

The cleaning robots, having carried out an automatic survey of the entire suite, rolled up to him and reported that the job was done. He dismissed them briskly, and the moment they had departed walked over to the nearest closet and commanded it to open. Horn, half-turning, gave a start.

"Why, it's full of Winch's belongings! Why didn't you tell Coolin to search them?''

24

"I formed my opinion of Coolin directly after his arrival," Dordy answered over his shoulder. "Shouldn't he have thought of doing that himself? It never occurred to him. As you just said, it's as though he doesn't really care. I formed my opinion of you in a hurry, too. It's a habit one has to learn in my job. I have to size up a client the moment I set eyes on him; there are some elements of 'good service' which no robotic device has yet been designed to cope with. And one carries the habit over into other areas, eventually."

Bewildered, never having heard an android speak so familiarly before, Horn watched as Dordy went on opening doors and drawers manually. Most of the compartments were empty; Winch must have brought much less baggage with him than the owner of the piled cases under which Latchbolt had been hidden.

At length, seeming satisfied, Dordy turned towards the door. On the threshold he paused, and gave Horn a long scrutinizing look, as though weighing him in a mental balance. He seemed to reach a crucial decision, though what it could be Horn hadn't the faintest idea.

"All right, Mr. Horn!" The words were stiff with tension. "Here's your chance to behave as though you mean what you've been talking about—to show you care as much about one of you with a knife in his heart as we do about one of us with his face beaten to pulp!"

He put his blue hand inside his dark tunic, fumbled in a pocket, and tossed something flat and oblong across the room to Horn, who caught it automatically.

"His name wasn't Winch," Dordy said. "His name was Lars Talibrand."

And he was gone.

Horn had been mechanically turning the thing he had been given over and over in both hands for long moments before he finally got around to looking at it. Considering the wealth and status of his family, he had had very little to do with androids most of his life—after all, the owners

25

of the planet's leading robot manufacturers could hardly employ other than their own much-touted products on their estate. But he had a distinct feeling that androids weren't supposed to act as Dordy had just been doing.

As soon as he started to examine his new acquisition, however, all such superficial thoughts vanished from his mind. What he held consisted in a sort of wallet of dull grey woven metal: a pocket-shaped sheath enclosing a smaller oblong which could be pulled out. He removed it. It was a thin booklet, the front cover engraved with words in five different languages. He could read only one of the various inscriptions—that in Anglic Terrestrial—but that was enough to make him blink with surprise.

This legend said, CITIZEN OF THE GALAXY.

Inside, a solido picture leapt up at him. It must have had bio-identity, for now it was fading from its original lifelike coloring towards a monotone grey, and the eyes in the face were closed. But enough detail remained for him to be certain this was the red-haired man who had died in this room.

Opposite the picture was a page of wording in an unfamiliar tongue, in the midst of which stood out the name Dordy had mentioned: "Lars Talibrand." The next page he could read, and was presumably a translation of the foregoing. It declared that on such a day of such a year the government of Creew 'n Dith had nominated Lars Talibrand to the distinction of galactic citizenship, and continued below in slightly different type to the effect that a world called Vernier had seconded the nomination, and again in yet another type added that a world called Lygos had confirmed it. At the foot of the page was a list of five other worlds to which the same Lars Talibrand had rendered signal service.

Horn felt a chill of awe run down his spine. What kind of a man was this who had died here? What kind of a man could do such work as to make whole planets grateful to him?

A man human enough to die when a knife was thrust

through his heart . . .

He got to his feet and determinedly set to, working his way through the sparse belongings in the room. He belatedly decided that it was for that purpose that Dordy had left all the drawers and closets ajar—otherwise only the registered occupant could have gained access to them unless he had one of the staff's pass-keys. There were a few changes of clothes, none suitable for the gaiety of carnival but all of them exotic to Earthly eyes: cracked leather breeches exuding alien scents, cleated boots, enormous enveloping parkas clearly destined for the climate of some world less thoroughly domesticated than this one. There were toilet articles, new, probably supplied by the hotel since his arrival. Nothing informative beyond that. Maybe the killer had already been through everything, though there was little to suggest hasty disturbance by a stranger.

Dissatisfied, he opened the booklet anew. He had presumed that it consisted entirely of versions of the same testimonial he had already read, in various languages. Now he found there were only as many translations as there were of the proud title on the cover—five. Behind followed pages and pages of planetary exit and entry stamps. He estimated two hundred or more, covering twenty different worlds, and the thought made him almost dizzy. A traveler, this man!

Curious, he glanced at the last page seeking an entry stamp for Earth. There wasn't one. But of course Coolin had been right in one thing: literally thousands of offworlders came to Earth at carnival time, and the authorities were then likely to grow lax.

He slid the booklet back into its wallet and set off in search of Dordy. He had a great many questions to ask.

CHAPTER IV

IN THE PUBLIC ELEVATORS the carnival spirit was already
rampant. A slender woman apparently wearing no more
than a coat of iridescent paint struggled to persuade him
to try a special euphoric she had been given, and on the
next stop down a grinning boy of sixteen or so entered
announcing his intention of spreading some *joie de vivre*
among the robots and androids on the service levels with
the help of a large carton of fireworks. Luckily for Horn,
who had much more serious business in the service
basement, the painted woman managed to press some of
her euphoric on the boy before he left the car, and the last
sight Horn had of him showed him sitting on the floor
with one elbow on his case of fireworks, lost in wave after
wave of helpless laughter.

Puzzled at finding a client in carnival dress in the
service basement, a robot inquired whether Horn had lost
his way. Shaking his head, he explained that he was
looking for Dordy's office.

Reproachfully the robot pointed out that he had only
to ask, and Dordy would come to his suite at the earliest
possible opportunity.

"I know what I'm doing!" Horn snapped. "Where is his
office, anyway?"

Programmed not to interfere with humans' decisions,
no matter how apparently irrational, unless lives were
being endangered, the robot gave up. "Third door on the
right, sir," it said. "But at present I do not believe he is
there."

Correct; the room was empty. Horn went in and sat
down in a hard plain chair, struck a smokehale and
prepared himself for a long wait. In fact, only a few
minutes had gone by when the door slid back again and
Dordy entered, betraying no surprise on seeing that he

28

had a visitor.

"I'm sorry you had to wait," he said. "I only just now saw the last of the lawforce androids off the premises. They were, as I think you realized, a little more thorough than Coolin."

"You sound—" Horn had to fumble for a word. "You sound defiant, Dordy!"

At that, the android did look surprised, and perhaps a trifle relieved. Shutting the door, he moved briskly to a chair facing Horn's.

"Yes, sir. 'Defiant' fits the case precisely. I suppose you refer to my use of unprefixed names for humans, for example 'Coolin' for 'Superintendent Coolin'?"

"I don't give a damn what you call him," Horn grunted. "I want to know more about *this*." He lifted the woven-metal wallet. "You intended me to come and ask questions about it, didn't you? I don't see any other reason for giving it to me."

Dordy nodded. "As I told you, sir, I reached a conclusion about you on very slender evidence. But sometimes one has to gamble. There are so many things a human can do which an android could—but can't. If you follow me."

Something in his tone made Horn want to apologize, but he had no idea why. He said gruffly, "Well, first off: I assume this is some kind of pass, or identity document. But I never heard of anyone being made a citizen of the galaxy before! What's it supposed to mean?"

"Such documents aren't recognized here," Dordy shrugged. "Earth is a curiously parochial world in some ways. But there's a lot more to the inhabited galaxy than just this one planet, as you'll have been reminded by the impressive array of entry and exit stamps in the back of that booklet."

"Yes, of course! I mean, one studies galactography in school, and gets to recognize the stars with inhabited planets in the sky at night. And there are imported luxuries and so on. Only ... only it doesn't mean very

29

much to most people, I guess."

"Apparently not, sir."

Was there sarcasm in the tone? If so, why? Horn felt a depressing sense of being at a loss, confronted with this blue-skinned inferior, and sternly reminded himself that after all Dordy wasn't even a naturally born man but only a facsimile grown from a programmed solution of organics in some elaborate fashion he did not know the details of. Men had invented the android process! Without human genius Dordy could never have come into existence.

It must have something to do with the universal phenomenon someone had once summed up by saying that no man is a hero to his valet. In Dordy's position there must be ample exposure to the foibles of humanity—more than enough to make him cynical and a little discourteous. No matter; a man, a real man, had died overhead a short while ago, and Derry Horn was not going to allow mere androids to display more concern over the death of one of their kind than humans did over the murder of one of theirs!

Determinedly, he plowed on with the questions he had in mind when he left Talibrand's suite.

"How did you come to get hold of this—this certificate?"

"Talibrand gave it to me on his arrival," said Dordy. "It was the most precious thing he had, except his life. He could only part with it because he knew he was in very great danger, and to have been found in possession of it would have sealed his fate however well he might otherwise have disguised his identity."

"But why to you?" Horn demanded. "Did you know him well?"

"I'd never seen him before."

"Then ..." No, this wasn't making sense. He tried another tack. "Who was he hiding from? Did he know someone was hunting him—did he know who? And if you know, why didn't you mention this to Coolin?"

"For the same reason I don't propose to tell you."

Dordy smiled.

"Then you do know!"

"I know nothing I could prove, *sir*." This time the irony was unmistakable. "I could name a name and feel certain it was right, and not be able to provide evidence in a hundred years."

"I think you're stalling," Horn said suddenly. "I think—yes, I see how it might be! It isn't anything to do with *me*, is it—not me personally? It's all because of your *friend* the floor manager who got killed! You saw me being sympathetic to him, and I guess you probably thought, 'Ah-hah! Here's Derry Horn, of Horn & Horn the rich robot manufacturers—if I play my cards right I can maybe get him to lean on the lawforce a bit and here's one android killing that won't get handled the way the law lays down'! I don't think you give a damn about Talibrand. I don't even believe he gave you this certificate of his. I think you probably took a quick look through his belongings before Coolin and his team got here, and made off with this because it might be important."

He tossed the grey wallet with its amazing booklet on to a nearby table, and got up.

"Well, I'm not going to be used, hear? It's the job of the lawforce to do whatever is to be done in a case like this, and if Coolin doesn't happen to be all that good at his work I'm shot if I'm going to make myself responsible for his failings! The hell with it all—I'm going out and have myself some fun!"

He was at the door when Dordy, who had not made a move, called after him.

"Mr. Horn!"

He glanced back, not speaking.

"You're wrong to say I don't care about Talibrand. He was a good man."

"Sure—that booklet says he was some kind of walking miracle! But in whose opinion? He wasn't anything to anyone on Earth."

"You're wrong there, too. Incidentally, there's no point

31

in leaving his pass with me. It's useless except to a human being. I can't do any good with it at all.''

"Nor can I," Horn said harshly, and went out.

A mobile fountain was rolling slowly past the entrance to the hotel when he reached the street. He hurried after it and swigged two or three mouthfuls of the various fruit-flavored euphorics streaming from its multiple spouts. At once a heady artificial gaiety took possession of him. He bought a mask from a passing vendor who had reserved the most resplendent of his creations for his own face, and ducked behind it into anonymity.

At the curb waited bubbletaxis, pastel-colored, lemon, pale green, pink, sky-blue. Their patient automatics hummed at the edge of audibility, awaiting passengers. As Horn strolled unhurriedly to select one for his own use, another which had been chartered elsewhere in the city settled to rest nearby, bearing a young couple making passionate love. Passers-by hooted with laughter at their annoyance as they perforce had to leave their vehicle and climb into the next in line to resume their airborne courtship. They took the one Horn had been intending to use. Gravely he bowed and gave them precedence, and the girl—it could be seen she was very pretty for she had removed her mask to make kissing easier—promised drunkenly that he could have her any time they met during the carnival, provided she was on her own.

It didn't seem likely.

He entered the bubbletaxi they had just vacated, and it took the air with a gentle bobbing motion, like a drifting feather. The seats were still warm from the former occupants, and a hint of fragrance clung even in the open cockpit. Horn put his feet up on the forward rim of the vehicle and leaned back to stare at the stars.

One learns to recognize the ones which have inhabited planets. . . .

Only later one also forgets, he qualified. He couldn't for the life of him have identified two of those stars and their

32

inhabited worlds. He could have listed most of the names, given a few minutes to think about them; what he could never have hoped to do was attach them all to the proper dots of brillance above.

Annoyed, he switched his attention to the lights underneath him instead. There was the fairground, over on his left; there was the arc of the beach, fringed with the luminous organisms sown at sundown, some of which had been carried out to sea in the wake of paddleboats or by chance changes in the current. His vehicle was bearing him in a wide curving swoop all over the city, controlled as much by the breeze as by its automatics. Now the air bore to him the distant fairground blare, now a freak snatch of song from a boat lazing on the ripples a mile from ashore. Carnival!

The sound montage should have been evocative, since it was part of the heritage of every living adult. It should at once, even without the euphorics he had gulped down, have snatched his imagination away from all such nastiness as androids beaten to death. Who cared about androids, anyhow—except other androids? And the man who had been killed was a total stranger, probably with delusions of grandeur to judge by the boastful certificate he had carried.

Yet, by the time his bubbletaxi had deposited him at the far edge of the fairground, in the thick of the merry-making, he was growing terrified at the prospect of being haunted for the whole of carnival week by visions of brutal murder. To distract himself he jumped out before the vehicle had properly come to rest and ran whooping down the grassy bank it had settled on to dive headlong between two gaudy concession-booths.

Two girls—alike, perhaps sisters—coming the other way arm-in-arm tried to leap apart in order to let him charge between them. They didn't quite separate fast enough, or he had to put his arms around them to save himself from falling, or something. However it might have been, a moment later they were all three sprawled on the ground in a tangle of limbs, kissing and laughing with the ring of hysteria that always pervaded the racket of carnival week.

"Get off me, idiot!" giggled one of the girls, seizing a discarded burr of glittering plastic from near at hand and tangling it among Horn's dark hair.

"Correct!" Horn declared. "I am an idiot! Carnival started hours ago, and I've only just turned up to join in! Want to help me make up for lost time?" He plucked at the hem of her skimpy dress while leering across her at her companion.

It took little persuasion. They linked arms again, this time with Horn in the middle, and went strutting through the fairground to a nonsense song picked up from one of the organs, to which each of them contributed a verse in turn. The girls seemed to laugh much louder at Horn's verses than at their own. Delighted, he laughed louder than both of them.

There were some performing shoemice from Vernier; they hooted with amusement over the antics of those. There was a not-quite-face on a purple animal from Lygos, which retained a perfectly solemn expression while its trainer drilled it through the most absurd contortions; that struck them as fantastically funny and left them barely able to stagger towards the next concession, where a lightning caricaturist turned each of them in turn into sarcastic parodies: the two girls into a kind of playing-card, heads and arms waving either side of a union at waist-height, and Horn into a hooded skeletal figure with a scythe. That was too appropriate to be amusing. He ripped the drawing of himself into shreds and chased the girls away, masking his annoyance with shrill cries of mock laughter. Balls of silver rising and falling in a shimmering column of light drew them; they found a device that distorted gravity at random and spent ten crazy minutes being whirled and tumbled together inside one of the balls ... after which the concessionaire discreetly allowed them a further ten minutes of privacy.

undisturbed.

Emerging thirsty, they stopped at a fountain. Horn had three measures, and thereafter the night began to melt together like a dream. They picked up other people along the way until he found himself leading a party of a dozen or more through sideshow after sideshow, competition after competition.

At last, though, it seemed that their gaiety was lessening while his still grew. Barely an hour remained before dawn. Some people were already asleep on the ground; this was usual on the first night of carnival. Tomorrow people would sleep all day and awake refreshed at sunset, whereas on this first day they would typically have been awake for twenty hours already.

"Come on!" Horn shouted hysterically. "We still haven't seen—"

And broke off, looking around rather foolishly. He was speaking to the air. His party had melted away. A sign on a neighbouring concesson offered a probable explanation. It read simply: DOUBLE BEDS.

All hilarity evaporated, and exhaustion took its place. He thought about the sign for a while, which was tempting even though neither of the sisters with whom he had begun the evening remained to keep him company; then he decided it was a waste when there was a comfortable hotel suite awaiting him. It would not be long before he could order a bubbletaxi to take him back to it. Meanwhile, he might as well sit down in one and let it bear him where it liked—it was more comfortable than sitting on the ground here. Not to mention cleaner; the ground was almost squelching with spilled liquor and perhaps less savory fluids, and all sorts of rubbish covered the grass.

He picked his way tiredly among the close-set booths, trying to remember when he had last gone to bed alone after a night of carnival, until he came to the place where bubbletaxis were parked. Just as he made to enter the nearest, there was a movement in shadow, and he drew back, gasping. One of the grey-clad Dispossessed had somehow managed to infiltrate the city, and was gazing straight at him with hungry, horrible eyes.

Nothing was said. There was only a look of accusation. But it hit him like an iron bar across the forehead. He stumbled backwards as the Dispossessed vanished into the darkness he had emerged from, and from behind him a voice said, "Clumsy fool!"

He was preoccupied for a moment with thoughts of the Dispossessed: condemned to the crudest, ugliest clothing, the barest of subsistence diets. He made no response.

The voice said again, "I called you a clumsy fool! And you are! I ought to run you through where you stand!"

Turning slowly, Horn realized he was being addressed by a stranger in gold and white, smeared with the marks of fruit where someone had pelted him for amusement. His face was hidden behind a gold mask, and his right hand rested on the hilt of a sword obviously meant for use and not for show.

Horn's heart seemed to congeal and sink to the bottom of his belly. In memory he could hear the voice of the pudgy man saying he hoped the sadist who had beaten Latchbolt to death would confine himself to androids during this carnival. He had heard of, but he had never before run across, those who would take advantage of the license of carnival to work off their desire for cruelty and bloodshed. That wasn't what dueling was meant for! It was only supposed to be a psychological prop—a subconscious reassurance for vigorous young men in a civilized society that if they had to they could fight to survive.

But even during carnival one didn't deliberately pick a quarrel with a total stranger for the sake of a fight! One enjoyed a few matches, perhaps picked up a few scars one might choose to keep if one felt it was glamorous . . .

Yet here was this stranger saying, in a voice which suddenly seemed as though it ought to be familiar, "Well? Is the clumsy fool going to behave decently and come with me to a dueling-hall, or must I simply stick him like a pig

36

out here in the open? Either way—are you listening?—I
propose to kill you.''

CHAPTER V

ALL OF A SUDDEN what traces of carnival mood remained
in Horn's mind, artificially supported by the various
euphorics he had continually gulped down since his
arrival at the fairground, vanished before a rising gale of
cold disgust. It had been threatening him all night, and he
had barely managed to hold it at bay; the starkness of the
stranger's words now stripped him of all defenses, and he
realized that without reservation he detested the world
that had bred him as he was.

For it had also spawned casual killers who could beat
androids to death for amusement, secure in the knowledge
that their crime was mere destruction of property. How
far above life was property prized, when the lack of it
condemned the losers to the living hell of Dispossession?

Waiting impatiently, the man in white and gold said.
'If I have to, I will run you through out here—I swear it!
And there will be no one but my *friends* as witnesses!''

Drawn back to the present, Horn looked about him. In
shadows nearby he detected blurred figures whose
attitude somehow betrayed eagerness. People of that kind
also were something he had heard about but not
encountered before: those who spent the week of carnival
tracking down sadistic killers and watching their duels
with a voyeur's greed. There were rules to govern dueling,
naturally, and such bystanders could always be relied on
to swear that they had been complied with.

He sought a way of escape, and realized sickly that
there was none. He could be tripped whichever way he
tried to run. Therefore . . .

Determination grew in him. Without realizing it, h
knew now that he had been surrounded all his life b
things which nauseated him. He had never struck back
but only hidden himself behind the stockade of securit
afforded by his grandfather's fortune. For better or worse
that was going to stop.

He saw that a cooler for iced drinks and confectioner
had been overturned a few paces from where he stood. H
strode towards it and slapped a handful of sticky bu
delightfully cold pulp on his forehead and cheeks. Hi
mask had long ago been mislaid in the tumult of the night
Refreshed, he turned to the man in white and gold.

"Very well. Where shall we go?"

The stranger took a step back, as though surprised t
find his challenge at last accepted. But he swiftl
recovered his self-possession.

"There is a hall a short distance from here which is stil
open. I see you have no sword of your own, but you ca
rent one there. Come with me."

Horn snatched up a blouse some girl had discarded o
the ground and used it to wipe away the last traces of th
fruit-pulp from his face. He was nervous, but to hi
amazement he was not afraid. He had conceived a sense o
purpose, though it was a purpose he intellectuall
despised, and the sensation was strange and somehov
inspiring. Falling in beside the challenger, he noticed fron
the corner of his eye that the anonymous watchers wer
following along behind.

"You seem to be pretty free with your challenges," h
muttered after a few paces. "Is the number of your kills i
the index of your enjoyment of carnival?"

The eyes behind the gold mask glinted. "I have killed a
every carnival since I was twenty!"

"By picking on opponents who have never bee
challenged before?" Horn made the words as insulting a
he could. The man in white and gold bridled.

"Once! Only once! Have you never dueled, then?"

"Not in your style, for the pleasure of a kill." Hor

38

hesitated, then decided the rest of the truth was worth exploiting for what it might do to undermine the stranger's arrogance. "But I won the premier award for swordplay in my home city last year."

And of course everyone assumed the family had bought the judges. . . . That was why he hadn't touched his sword in eight months, why he had left it at home instead of bringing it with him for carnival week. Acquiring that skill had been the only thing in his life he had ever taken really seriously; then when he found how people regarded his triumph the whole of his enthusiasm had turned to ashes.

With melancholy satisfaction he noted that the news seemed to have the desired effect on his companion. The man did not utter another word until they had entered the dueling-hall.

There was no one else present except the concessionaire, drowsing over his reception desk, and cleaning robots were waiting in the corners ready to sweep up the bloodstained sand scattered on the floor and replace it with fresh for the next night's custom. Briefly Horn's resentment against the universe sought a focus in the proprietor—what sort of man could bring himself to spend carnival week offering facilities for violent death?—but a moment later he found himself wondering whether it might not be a real service for some people whose *ennui* had reached the stage where even suicide appeared pointless, and who might welcome the chance to have a limit set to the emptiness of their lives.

Passively, he agreed for the benefit of the record that he had been properly challenged by the man in white and gold. One of the masked "friends" of the latter who had accompanied them into the hall emerged from anonymity long enough to confirm the statement before joining his companions, all hooded and cloaked, in a group at the side of the hall.

"I'll have to rent a sword," Horn grunted when the legalities were over. "Have you a Duple Champion?"

"Of course, sir," the proprietor sighed, and produced one from a rack of weapons behind his desk. Horn felt it, tried a pass or two—which told him that he was slow through lack of practice—and applied it to the whirring grindstone beside the weapons rack. Stroking a few grains of metal from the thickest part of the blade turned it into the counterpart of his own at home, perfectly balanced.

But one difference did remain. This was keener than a razor, whereas his own was blunt.

"Anywhere you like on the floor, gentlemen," the proprietor said. "I don't expect we shall have anyone else in before dawn."

That at least would be a help, Horn thought: not to be hemmed into the standard dueling-zone by the tingling beams of light-bars. If all else failed him, he could at least retreat and retreat until this stranger so eager for a kill grew bored and relaxed his concentration.

And yet ...*stranger?* Once more he had the curious sensation he had felt when he was first challenged; that he ought to be able to place the man in white and gold.

But there was no time to wonder about such superficialities. The challenger had squared off and the automatic countdown had begun. A small black cloud of nervousness had formed behind Horn's eyes, which he could foresee growing larger if he was indeed forced to stretch the contest unduly. Make it quickly, then, if at all possible— make it before the other man began to recognize with his muscles as well as his mind that his opponent had exceptional skill.

They touched blades on the instant the countdown ended, parried, twisted and broke free, getting each other's measure. Horn knew he was the slower after ten short seconds; yet in the same span of time, with dawning astonishment, he realized something else which was so much to his advantage he hardly dared act on it. The stranger was no longer his own master—hadn't been since the first click of their blades. He was instantly in the grip of blood-lust, and his next move was to launch a frenzied

40

attack as though determined to hack Horn limb from limb.

Dimly at the remote edge of the consciousness fined down to absolute concentration on the fight, Horn caught the sound of a unison sigh of—pleasure? relief?—something crazily askew from normality, anyhow, uttered by the faceless cluster of watchers who had come in the hope of seeing a man die in slow agony. He decided that he was not going to pander to that unnatural lust any longer than was necessary. And in fact the time was so short he barely believed it even when the duel was over.

The challenger, carried away, overreached himself. In the fraction of a second when the trick was safe, Horn employed the same device which had won his championship match the year before, changed hands on his sword and stroked the tip up his opponent's body from crotch to rib-cage. At the end of its course he thrust it home and let it go.

His belly opened like a half-peeled banana, the man in white and gold reeled backward and slumped gurgling to the floor. Horn didn't bother to look at his work. He merely headed for the door.

Goggle-eyed, the proprietor hurried from the desk to bar his way, demanding who was going to pay his fee. Horn shrugged.

"He challenged me! Let him pay, whoever he is!"

Who *was* he, anyway? Fighting nausea at the sight of his third corpse within twenty-four hours, and a still stronger wave of it due to his half-awareness of the disappointment the watchers were exuding at the shortness of the fight, he returned to strip the mask from the face of the dead man.

No wonder the voice had struck a chord in memory, although now he realized it had been disguised with deliberate deepness and an affected formality of speech.

He had killed Superintendent Coolin of the lawforce.

Restlessly, Horn tossed in his superbly comfortable

41

bed. He was physically exhausted—the tension of the duel had drained during his return to the hotel and left all his limbs numb—but he could not dig his way into the dark mine of sleep. It was not merely that whenever his eyes were closed he saw visions of Latchbolt's face, beaten into ruin; of Talibrand's, composed and hideously vacant; of Coolin's, contorted in agony; and that these images would inevitably haunt his dreams.

It was simply that he could not foresee himself ever sleeping soundly again on a world which committed responsibility for the maintenance of law and order into the hands of a man who could boast of having killed at every carnival since he was twenty.

What had attracted Coolin into his job, anyhow? The chance of being able to feast his eyes every now and then on the consequences of a rare crime of violence?

That question was unanswerable, at least so long as carnival went on.

At length the little booklet belonging to Talibrand floated into his mind's eye, and he saw the pages turn to reveal proof of visits to one after another of the worlds that had later attested their gratitude in that amazing certificate at the beginning of the document. What could this Lars Talibrand have done? What could Derry Horn dream of doing that might be equally honoured and praised? Certainly nothing that belonged to the pattern his grandfather had mapped out for him, which he had scarcely questioned since he grew old enough to talk.

That elderly autocrat had certainly accomplished a great deal in his long life. He had supplied the population not only of Earth but of several outworlds with more, and more efficient, robots than any competitor. They might not be as versatile as androids, but they were far more reliable, and immune from the almost human nervous breakdowns which occasionally afflicted very highly strung specimens of android. (Not that these ever went so far as violent outbursts against their owners—there was a guarantee in all contracts of sale that the worst which would happen was catatonic withdrawal from reality.)

Yet was this commercial achievement anything likely to bring him recognition as a universal benefactor, a "citizen of the galaxy"? Of course not. He already had all the benefits he could imagine, and in his old age he was growing crotchety—so his grandson had often suspected —through lack of new incentives.

What would happen when the old tyrant got to hear of the events of the past day? Probably he'd take his grandson severely to task, like a schoolboy, for being so stupid as to get mixed up in things which didn't concern him. Then he would probably make some inquiries and grease a few palms by way of insurance for the family's good name, and nothing more would ever be heard of the affair.

His father? He'd probably offer gruff compliments on the victory over Coolin and then go see *his* father in a fit of agitation about possible complications. His mother, on the other hand, would certainly flutter woollily about him risking his life, before going away and boasting of her boy's fighting skill to her friends.

His sister, who was four years younger than he, would perhaps have another fit of that wide-eyed hero worship he had basked in until a year or two ago. By now, though, she was likely to be growing out of it, having found it as pointless as he had already decided. And, according to their ages, the rest of the family—of whom there were seemingly myriads scattered across the face of Earth— would either loudly wonder what the younger generation could be coming to these days, or scornfully condemn the exhibitionism of their relative, keeping their envy of him secret.

Last afternoon he had been dismayed at the prospect of not enjoying carnival this year. It was infinitely worse to find himself not expecting to enjoy the rest of his life.

The sun was high in the sky, invisible behind the opaqued windows of his suite, when he at last managed to doze off into unrestful slumber. When he awakened, he

43

knew the instant he opened his eyes not only that someone had been into his room while he slept, but who that person was.

Dordy.

For, on the table beside him where he had left nothing but a pack of smokehales and a kerchief when he went to bed, there now also reposed the grey wovenmetal wallet which had belonged to Lars Talibrand.

He sat up, ordered the windows to clear, struck a smokehale and slipped the booklet out of the wallet again, thumbing the pages. The names of the many worlds on which Talibrand had been a welcome guest rang in his head as he studied them.

What were they like? He had been told, doubtless, many times in school; now he had to corrugate his brow in an effort to unite facts with names, almost as he had done last night when looking up from the bubbletaxi at the stars. Creew 'n Dith: something about the sound suggested sharp cold gales blasting around a fastness on the crest of a mountain. Arthworld: again, this had evocative echoes, like waves breaking on the sand of a long white beach ...

All that, out there! Millions of individuals with personal identities, ruling, serving, loving, hating, doing all the human things—but not as he himself did them, at one well-cushioned remove from reality. The thought caused a wrenching change in his mental perspective, as though something had kicked his awareness off down a path at right angles to its accustomed one. He pictured Earth, the parent world, as a dowager like his deceased great-grandmother, content to relax and play with her lapdogs while her son went out and carved himself a financial empire to keep her in luxury.

Now this man Talibrand ...

He turned to the solido at the beginning of the booklet. It had faded to uniform greyness now. Lars Talibrand was finished. Only ... well, if he had made himself so important that enemies hunted him from world to world, and even to Earth where his safe-conduct of galactic citizenship no longer protected himself, then the chances were that he must have been equally keenly loved, and have left behind countless thousands of friends.

The beginnings of a decision sprouted in Horn's mind, like a shy flower putting forth green to test the climate of spring. He turned to the last page of the booklet on which planetary entry stamps appeared, and his eyes unfocused as he looked beyond the printed name to the reality it implied.

Newholme. A nice substantial name, that. Without the romantic ring of Creew 'n Dith or Lygos. But different from the flat, placid, plopping sound *Earth*.

The decision hardened, and he spent a brief moment wondering in bewilderment whether this was what Dordy had been obliquely referring to yesterday, and how a mere android could foresee something in the mind of a man before the man himself was aware of it.

That, though, was of no consequence. He was going to Newholme.

CHAPTER VI

A HEADY EXCITEMENT seized him, tempered with not a little anxiety. But also there was impatience, to the point where he felt every second he spent after making up his mind was the waste of a chance to leave Earth. He leapt from the bed shouting for service, telling the robot which answered his call to bring him breakfast and fetch Dordy to his suite.

Showered and dressed faster than ever before in his life, he was gobbling down a hasty meal when the android acting-manager finally entered, looking extremely tired.

"You sent for me. Mr. Horn? I'm sorry to have taken so long, but during carnival this place is—well . . ." A shrug completed the apology.

"Never mind," Horn said out of a full mouth. "I just wanted to let you know I'm checking out."

Dordy nodded. "You've found more congenial accommodation for the rest of carnival? With friends, perhaps? Or *a* friend?"

"I'm sick of carnival!" Horn gave the words a measured emphasis. "I'm sick of the people who take part. I'm sick of the things they do. I'm getting the hell out."

"Yes, sir. It's still carnival week for everyone else, though."

Horn froze for an instant as the implication sank in. Of course! It would be pretty nearly impossible to go anywhere for the remaining six days. People weren't expected to want to travel during this season—they were supposed to be too busy enjoying themselves. Then he relaxed. There'd be a way of getting around that difficulty. There was always some way of getting around any difficulty.

"Never mind that for the moment! Sit down. I thought you might be interested to hear what made up my mind for me."

With an expression of polite interest Dordy complied and Horn went on, "Someone challenged me to a duel just before dawn. I killed him."

"As though there hadn't been enough deaths already," Dordy said, his pose of civility slipping. He tried and failed to master a yawn. Deliberately appearing to miss the point, Horn shook his head.

"Not for him apparently. It was Coolin, the lawforce superintendent."

The blue skin above Dordy's right eye wrinkled as he raised the eyebrow. "Really! Well, that explains quite a lot of things."

"Does it for you? It leaves me completely in the dark,"

46

Horn said in an aggrieved tone. "What exactly does this news—ah—clarify for you?"

"I'm sorry, sir." Dordy palmed his eyes and rubbed the skin of his temples, as though stretching it. "I'm very tired, and it would be dreadfully complicated to try and explain everything right now." He dropped his hands. "But I ought at least to give you a warning. It was bad luck for you to get mixed up in the murder of Lars Talibrand. If you'd behaved like an average citizen—given your testimony and shown impatience to get on with the fun of carnival—you'd probably not have been bothered again. By doing more than this minimal civic duty, you've probably marked yourself out as a potential danger to a lot of very dangerous people."

"But—but this sounds like a historical melodrama!" Horn objected.

"Isn't it dramatic that a man should have been hounded from planet to planet, driven out of the regions where his reputation protected him to Earth where his immunity no longer held good—and killed?"

"That's not just something you worked out from looking at the booklet you gave me. You sound far too positive." Horn thrust back his chair from the breakfast-table. "How do you come to know so much about this Lars Talibrand whom you claim never to have met before he checked in at your hotel?"

"What you really mean is: how does a menial android come to know more of what's going on in the galaxy than—No, I'm sorry. I oughtn't to say something like that. I can only promise you that you could learn exactly the same facts as I know if you took the trouble to go and look for them."

"I'm going to," Horn said determinedly.

There was a long pause. At last Dordy said, in a voice absolutely different from the tone he ordinarily affected, the deferential one suited to an android on the staff of a luxury hotel, "Then I wish you luck, Mr. Horn. You'll need it. It would be a brave thing for a man to expose

47

himself—like an android—to the risk of death without retribution from the law.''

Horn froze. In the words he seemed to hear the tolling of a funeral bell, or a dreadful sentence being uttered in the court of the universe. But before he could speak again. Dordy had risen and resumed his subordinate manner.

"I'll arrange to have your baggage at the exit directly you find transport for yourself, Mr. Horn. I hope you succeed in doing so.''

A few hours later, sheer frustration was bringing Horn around to the conclusion that Dordy, in spite of being a lowly android, was possessed of far more common sense than he was. He had come equipped with enough money and credit certificates to last him through carnival, and a return ticket to his home city so that even if he managed to exhaust his stock of cash he could still get home. But the ticket, naturally, was useless—no public transport except bubbletaxis operated during carnival week—and even those owners of vehicles in whom his offer of payment woke a flicker of cupidity admitted that they had time-locked the controls for fear of gambling or giving their property away. Everyone else, better adjusted to their world than these few with faults they recognized, laughed at him. They were as well off already as they could imagine being; a few thousand credits made small difference one way or another.

Certainly the money wouldn't repay them for the loss of a whole night of carnival.

At sunset, when there was no longer a chance of stopping a sober person on the street and striking a bargain because the entire adult population was hurrying to the fairground or to private parties, Horn made his way morosely back to the hotel. The money he had with him, he had lately realized, was on the one hand too much— since in this mood he was never going to spend it on carnival amusements—and on the other far too little, for it would barely cover the price of even a one-way ticket from Earth to Newholme. He had learned this from a tariff-board displayed outside an interstellar travel agency. The office beyond, of course, was shut.

Despondently, on returning to his suite, he sent for Dordy, with a vague idea that the android might honor his credit certificates and let him have extra cash so that tomorrow he could try the effect of increasing his offer for the loan of a vehicle. Almost as soon as the robot had departed to fetch him, the acting-manager appeared at the door of the suite.

"Ah, Mr. Horn! You've had no luck, I judge from your expression! But don't worry—I haven't cleared your baggage or re-allotted your rooms."

"Damnation!" Horn exclaimed. "Nobody gives a hoot for anything but this lunatic carnival right now! You'd think the world had come to a complete stop!" The implications of this last remark penetrated, and he put his hand on his chin, musing. "But it can't have, can it? There must always be some services which have to continue—power, and water-supply, and heating, and even maintenance of the carnival gear like bubbletaxis and fountains when someone decides to bash them about. And I guess the lawforce has to keep going, too; carnival isn't a season of *complete* lawlessness. Who the hell takes care of all that?"

Dordy just stood there and looked at him.

"Yes, of course," Horn said finally. "It was a damned stupid question, wasn't it? But . . ." He gathered courage; this somehow demanded more of him than accepting Coolin's challenge had required last night, even though his life was not at stake. "Look—ah . . . sit down! Smoke?" He proffered his pack of smokehales.

Dordy accepted the chair, but waved the smokehales aside. "Not allowed, sir," he said. "We're conditioned against them, in fact. And against liquor and all euphoric and depressant drugs."

Horn made to set one to his own lips, then realized that to someone who was immune from the taste for such

49

things the sight of a man sucking grey vapor out of a thin white tube was probably rather ridiculous. He changed his mind and instead voiced the idea which had just occurred to him.

"Well, anyway! I've had no luck in trying to borrow or rent a vehicle to get me home, so I was wondering—ah— whether any of your people could organize a heli for me Or something. I mean, since you're temporarily in charge ..." The words trailed away, but he had made his point.

"You had it in mind to offer payment?" Dordy said.

"Why, of course. I'd pay generously."

"No doubt, sir." Dordy sounded patient. "I was just wondering whether you expected your money to be desirable to—as you put it—one of my people. Androids are not permitted to spend money in public places, nor do they enjoy the advantages of credit rating. Bluntly, sir even though I grant that it is possible for one android to be better off than another, it is wholly impossible for any android to be better off than any human being. So money is, so to say, irrelevant."

Embarrassed at not having deduced the consequences of a fact he was perfectly aware of, Horn said harshly "Not better off than the Dispossessed?"

"Dispossession lasts a maximum of two years, sir Being an android is"—Dordy gestured as though feeling for a word in the air before him—"permanent."

"Hell's bells!" Horn exclaimed. A half-remembered tag from a history text crossed the field of his memory, and he grabbed at it. "Then how about—what's it called?— manumission? You know, release from a service contract My family is pretty well off. I'm sure I could arrange for any android who helped me to be bought from his present owner and—and turned loose."

"To do what?" Dordy said. He sounded tense, as though trespassing over the limits laid down by his status in life, prepared at any moment to be told to shut up and get out. "Androids get their freedom by doing, Mr. Horn What do you think I would say if someone—let' postulate a customer of the hotel who was particularly pleased with the service I'd organized during his stay—bought me out and said, 'Dordy, you can quit your job and there's no need for you to work ever again'? I'd thank him kindly and turn the offer down. What would I do if I lost this job? Sit on my bunk in an android barracks and read the classics of literature?"

He waved the notion aside, looking faintly bored. "But never mind that, sir. Suppose you tell me exactly what you're hoping to do?"

There was a long silence. Eventually words emerged from Horn's mouth which he himself heard with vague astonishment.

"I guess—I guess I don't really know. It started with the idea that someone ought to bring to justice the man who killed Talibrand, and your floor manager too. But that's ridiculous. It's straight out of a historical romance. I guess I'd be satisfied to get up there, the other side of our nice clear blue sky, and discover what a man could do to be nominated as a citizen of the galaxy. I'd just plain like to be convinced that things of that kind still exist. Beyond that, I . . ." He turned his hand over, palm to the floor, and scowled.

"I'm told that life on worlds other than Earth isn't so comfortable as here, sir," Dordy said.

"So what?" Horn jumped to his feet and began to pace the room. "I'm wealthy without having asked to be—it just happened when I was born! And I'm miserable! Damn it. I am! I don't have any purpose in living, never have had, ever seem likely to have! *I'm* never going to have a job like yours where someone might one day come along and say, 'Well done, I want to pay you back for everything!' I'm just going to occupy the well-worn grooves of a career laid down for me before my father got married, and when I die no one will be able to remember whether I did this or that, or whether my father or my grandfather worked it all out and just ordered me to get on with it. And I can't stand it any longer!"

51

Dordy seemed to be debating within himself. After a while he too got up, straightening his smart formal clothing with quick twitches.

"In that case, Mr. Horn, you needn't worry any longer about your transport. It's waiting for you as soon as you're ready to leave."

CHAPTER VII

IN DORDY'S OFFICE was a big taciturn android with a blunt chin, wearing the coarse overalls of a general service technician. As Horn, still trying to make sense of what had happened, accompanied Dordy into the room, this android rose automatically to his feet, then gave him a searching look and switched his eyes to Dordy.

"Him?" he said in a neutral tone that came within an ace of being disparaging.

"Yes, of course!" Dordy snapped. "Mr. Horn, this is Berl. He's with the municipal service department. He's off duty tonight, and has access to a heli in which he can take you home."

Uncomfortable, Horn said, "Well, there isn't any need for that, you know. I can fly a heli if you can loan one to me."

"With all the continental guide-beams turned off for overhaul?" Berl grunted, and added belatedly, "Sir!"

"Why—no! I mean, are they? I didn't realize."

"Sure they are. Carnival's the best chance we get to withdraw public service equipment from regular use and check it out. At that there's a lot of work to cram into one week, even working around the clock. Maybe it would be a good idea to double the length of carnival, give a bit more elbow-room."

There was a faint hissing sound from beyond the door

...hen a sharp report, and a crash as though a pile of crocks had been dropped. "Excuse me," said Dordy wearily, and went to see what had happened. Horn waited for his return, very conscious of Berl's scrutiny but unable to say anything.

Dordy was only out for a short time, however, and came back with a frown. "Boy with some fireworks," he announced. "He was here last night too—full of the carnival spirit. He blew the foot off a robot waiter with that one. I hope his family can stand the bill they're going to get next week! What was that you were saying about wanting carnival to go on longer, Berl?"

The blue-skinned men exchanged glances full of mutual comprehension; Horn felt oddly left out of the exchange. Then Berl shrugged.

"Well, life's like that. Okay, Mr Horn, let's go. You won't find my heli very comfortable, I'm afraid—the only place I could borrow from was the wreck-salvage section. But it has just been thoroughly checked, so you can rely on it getting you where you want to go."

Horn turned awkwardly to Dordy. "I don't quite know how to say thanks," he muttered. "You told me money isn't any good, but if there's anything at all I can—"

Dordy raised his hand. "Androids don't have to be thanked any more than they have to be paid, Mr. Horn. You just go where that booklet of Lars Talibrand's leads you. You can do it. I wouldn't be allowed to."

Berl gave a sound halfway between a grunt and a laugh, and waited impatiently by the door for Horn to join him.

"But—" Horn felt briefly giddy. "But you *know* where, don't you? You know what Lars Talibrand's work was! Why won't you tell me?"

"Because you don't have to walk out of that door, sir. The moment you do, you'll be in it up to your neck, and from then on it will be up to you whether you come out with your life. Goodbye, Mr. Horn."

The heli Berl had borrowed was indeed a long way from

53

the Passenger models to which Horn was accustomed. Potbellied, immensely powerful, it lumbered through the sky at a slow hundred and fifty with its unretracted legs spread wide on either side of its folded grappling equipment. He sat in acute discomfort on a plain metal bench which doubled as a toolchest—the tools rattled like the chains of a banshee every time the engine hit a particular frequency—beside what struck him as an appallingly flimsy door fitted with a catch Berl sternly warned him not to touch or even brush against while they were moving, for fear it might spring open.

The square edge of his seat cut off the circulation in his legs, sending his calves to prickling sleep no matter how often he tried to shift his weight from one side to the other. There was a stink of lubricant from the bearings of the rotor overhead.

"It's not designed for this sort of trip," Berl vouchsafed after they had been in flight nearly an hour. He seemed to be half amused and half sympathetic towards Horn's vain attempts to make himself comfortable. But it was the first thing he had said without prompting since they set out; to Horn's halting remarks about the advantages and drawbacks of carnival, uttered earlier, he had returned only grunts and nods.

It was cold up here; Horn leaned back to make the most of what warmth seeped through from the engine astern of their cockpit.

"Ah—what exactly is this machine designed for then?" He ventured. "Didn't you say something about borrowing it from the wreck-salvage section?"

"That's right," Berl nodded. There was no light except from the stars and the dim glow of the instrument panel; the blueness of his skin was turned to a grey as neutral as was Horn's own complexion. "All I could get was this heavy lifting job, y'see. Rest of the helis are due for major overhauls. Take days, maybe all of what's left before carnival is through. But this type doesn't see too much service during an average year, doesn't get worn out so quick. It's the kind you send out when a couple of groundcars get so tangled up in an important intersection you can't risk waiting till you've cut 'em into sections the small helis can handle. Ever seen one of them at work?"

"No, I don't believe I ever have," Horn said. "I've been by at a spot where accidents like that had recently happened, I think, but it was always cleaned up before I arrived. I guess—" He hesitated, couldn't decide why, and finished what he had been about to say. "I guess you boys do a pretty fast job!"

"We try to. Right now, of course, we can take things easy—you can't do much harm if you break a bubble-taxi, and all it needs is to send out a mechanic in a floater. The rest of the year, though, you keep us pretty busy."

He didn't sound in the least resentful—rather, his tone was one of satisfaction, as though he was glad of the demands his job made on him. Nonetheless he fell silent again, and there was an interval during which the only sound was the drone of the rotors. Horn, peering overside, spotted the lights of a city to the east, which he could not identify: a patch of misty brilliance like an extra-galactic nebula viewed through a giant telescope, dotted with occasional brighter points like novae. He commented on the resemblance to Berl, not wanting to let the conversation die, but the android only shrugged.

"Wouldn't know about that. My job's wreck-salvage."

Am I crazy? Horn asked himself. *To think of leaving Earth on some wild chase among the outworlds, when there's so much right here at home I know nothing about?*

But it was too late for second thoughts. Berl was throttling back the power and the heli was losing height. A group of lights ahead suddenly took on familiar patterns. That was the Horn family's estate, and they were about to land. He realized with dismay that he hadn't planned what he was going to say to his relatives, rehearsed counters to their predictable objections.

Well, he would probably still have time to think about that. It was hours before dawn. The whole family was

55

probably scattered over a hundred square miles, and before his father came home he could expect plenty of opportunity to sit and muse by himself.

The heli touched down. Berl reached across him and flipped the catch of the passenger door. It dropped to form a ramp for exit. Stiffly rising to scramble out, Horn muttered automatic thanks, and instantly re-heard Dordy's cynical remark that androids didn't have to be thanked any more than they had to be paid.

"Say—uh—Mr. Horn!"

Turning, he saw Berl leaning down from the high doorway of the heli.

"Dordy told me you have Lars Talibrand's certificate. Is that right?"

Horn clapped his palm to the pocket in which he had slipped the document. It was where it ought to be. He nodded.

"Well—uh . . ." Berl seemed oddly at a loss. "Could I see it? Just for a moment?"

"Why—why, sure!" Bewildered, Horn produced it and handed it over. There was a pause. He could just discern the android's fingers turning the pages in the dim glow of the instrument lights.

Then the document was being extended for him to retrieve, and Berl was saying in a tone absolutely unlike any of his previous remarks, "Thank you, sir! I really appreciate that!"

What? I'm the one who's been done a favor, surely! But while Horn was still fumbling for words Berl had closed the door and fed power to the rotors. Battered by the vertical gale, he turned and trudged towards the house; before he reached it, the heli was out of sight.

He had been set down on the rear lawn among beds of night-scented flowers which ordinarily perfumed the whole vicinity of the house. The heli had left behind so strong a reek of hot oil, however, that it was still in his nostrils when a hand-held flashlight sprang up ahead of him and a quiet, familiar voice said, "Good morning, Mr.

Derry. Welcome home."

"Thanks, Rowl. Uh—you don't seem very surprised to see me back." Horn fell in alongside the portly android butler who had been in his family's service since he was first imported. He had heard—but only at second-secondhand—of the argument which had raged about employing an android in the household of the planet's leading robot manufacturer, no matter how fallible those robots had been thirty years ago. The disagreement had been settled on the basis that it must be an *imported* android, whose prestige value would perhaps compensate for the obvious drawbacks. Nonetheless, Rowl was still the only android on the staff; the rest were custom-designed robots.

"Well, no, Mr. Derry," Rowl said. "You see, the manager's secretary called me from the hotel where you were staying and warned me of your impending arrival."

"Did he now!" Horn checked in mid-stride, briefly possessed of a vague sense that he had been left out of something, his imagination tantalised by a half-formed vision of a planet-embracing network of androids, a colossal grapevine of news and gossip. But he had known Rowl since his birth; far too many years of childhood memory conspired against his thinking of the butler in any other than the ordinary context of his home. At a loss for the latest of uncountable times since the start of carnival, he peered into the house through the transparent walls which in summer gave the illusion of continuity between living-area and gardens, seeing no movement except that of the ever-busy cleaning robots.

"Well, that was thoughtful of him," he said at last. "Ah—is anyone else at home?"

"No, sir. Mr. Derry senior went to a party last night and did not return, though he is expected not to remain away indefinitely, and Mrs. Lu"—his mother—"said that . . ." Rowl gave a discreet cough, letting the words tail away.

"Said that if he could do it so could she and she won't be back tonight." Horn snorted. "You don't have to be tactful with me, Rowl!"

"I suppose not, sir," Rowl admitted, looking pained nonetheless at the accuracy of Horn's guess. "Well, anyway: Mr. Horn"—his grandfather, who as head of the family alone rated the formal use of its surname—"has been saying he doesn't enjoy carnival as much as he used to. He was in a very bad temper when he returned yesterday morning, and I regret to say I expect he will probably feel the same today."

"What about my sister?"

"Oh, Miss Via is with a party of students under the supervision of your cousin Mrs. Leadora. That entire branch of the family is here, incidentally."

"Damn. I'd clean forgotten about their being invited for the week. Oh well, never mind—I shan't be around long enough to be pestered by them, with luck. Rowl, do you suppose there's a hundred thousand in ready cash in the house?"

"Well ... yes, sir, there is indeed. But of course the ordinary expenses of carnival will substantially reduce that sum during the next few days."

"Let'em have their fun on credit, then! If a Horn can't command credit, who on this horrible planet can? I'm going to need cash—a lot of it—in a hurry! Here, get me a drink and a snack, will you? I need it to set me up for an argument with grandad."

If Rowl had the faintest inkling why his employer's grandson wanted so much money in a hurry, he didn't betray the fact, but merely bowed and moved to comply.

CHAPTER VIII

HE ATE sitting alone on the long central lounge which ran from end to end of the house, his back to the transparent wall fronting the garden, as though the world beyond held too many problems for him to feel comfortable looking at it. His appetite was long ago sated, and he had called on Rowl for several more drinks, before the hours of waiting were over and the peace of the house was shattered by the irruption of his sister Via at the head of a score of shrieking teenagers, with his mother's elderly cousin Leadora vainly struggling to quiet them.

The moment she saw her brother, Via rushed forward with a cry. "Derry, you beast! You've lost my bet for me!"

"What bet?" Horn said crossly.

"Oh, I told Sampidge that you'd enjoy carnival so much better on your own that you wouldn't come back until you absolutely had to. And he said you would come home early because it's much more fun to spend carnival with people you know, and here you are back already so I'll have to let him do all kinds of awful things to me and you're a beast! You're an absolute and utter *beast!*"

"You ought to be more careful who you make bets with, then," Horn snapped, pushing her aside as she made to pummel him and rising to his feet. "But don't worry— your bet's a washout, anyway. I haven't come back to spend the carnival with people I know. I've just come to pick up some cash so I can buy a flight to Newholme."

"Where's that?" Via said foggily. "Is it far?"

At that moment there was a lull in the chatter and laughter which had filled the room, and Horn's harsh reply was loud enough to be heard by everyone.

"Far? It's a pretty long way from Earth, but it's hardly far enough!"

Heads turned on all sides to look at him. A boy of about eighteen with a scholarly manner detached himself from the group of young people he had been talking to and approached Horn—Sampidge, who had made the bet with Via.

"Did I hear you say you were leaving Earth? Isn't the middle of carnival an odd time to get the pioneering

59

spirit?"

Horn scowled at him. He had no idea what Via's bet with Sampidge had involved, but on a brief acquaintance he had conceived an acute dislike for him and was prepared to make some cynical guesses.

"Pioneering spirit has nothing to do with it," he said. "It's just that I've finally figured out it would be easier to book one passage on a starship than rid this planet of all the people like you who make it unbearable!"

"Hoity-toity!" Sampidge began, bridling, but at that moment someone in the background, already bored with the distraction offered by Horn's outburst, picked up a fat cushion from the long lounge and threw it at Sampidge. It missed and hit Via, who hurled it back with a shriek, and in another few seconds there was a first-class mock fight in progress, from which Horn gratefully withdrew into a corner, reflecting sourly on the all-too-real fight he had himself become involved in exactly one day ago.

Then a rasping voice cut through the racket. "What the hell is all this? Rowl, clear these young ruffians out of here!"

Silence fell instantly, like night on an airless world. Shamefacedly, the teenagers abandoned the cushions they were flinging around, muttered, "Good morning, sir!" like so many androids, and made themselves scarce, Via and Sampidge along with the rest.

As they passed him in the doorway, Grandad Horn favored each of them with a scowl. The same look was still on his face when he finally spotted his grandson at the side of the room.

"Derry? What the hell are you doing here? I thought you'd taken it into your empty head that our company wasn't good enough for you this carnival—what are you doing back so soon? Rowl, get me a drink!"

He marched forward and carefully folded his aged legs on the edge of the long lounge.

"I've decided this kind of company isn't good enough for me—period!" Horn said, the anger he would have directed at Sampidge and his sister making the words fiercer than he had intended. "I want the fare to leave Earth!"

Rowl appeared with the drink Grandad Horn had requested—the old man had long ago conceded that when it came to personal service none of his robots could match their android butler—and was waved aside.

"Derry, you're either out of your head, or . . .ah-hah! I get it!" The old man leaned back, chuckling. "Who was she? Must have been quite a dish to take away your taste for carnival!"

"I'm not mooning over a woman!" Horn blazed. "I'm just fed up with Earth, and—and I have something to do out there behind the sky!"

His grandfather's near-century of age sat lightly on him. He had often taken advantage of that to attempt brotherly confidences with his grandson. Now, in spite of all the previous disasters this habit had led to, he tried again. Patting the cushion beside him, he said, "Come and sit down, Derry. Never let it be said I don't have time to solve my family's problems for them."

The arrogance of that made Horn angrier still. He remained defiantly where he was.

"Very well!" His grandfather finally reached for the drink Rowl had brought him and took a swig of it. "But at least tell me what's happened!"

"Well, last night I killed someone," Horn began. "A lawforce superintendent named Coolin—"

But his grandfather had leapt ahead of him. "That's not good, young fellow—not good at all! A lawforce superintendent! What did he do, pick on you unjustly in a crowd or something?"

"Sure he picked on me. Forced me to a dueling hall. He—"

"You beat him in a regular duel? Hell, boy, that's not something to be ashamed of—it's something to be *proud* of! And everyone's equal during carnival, no matter who they are for the rest of the year!" Mentally the old man was slapping shut the well-filled pocketbook he would have had to draw on otherwise.

From outside there came the noise of a heli descending. The old man cocked his head on one side. "Rowl! Who's that turning up here at this time of night?"

"Mr. Derry senior, sir," the butler said. "At least I presume so—it's the model of heli which he uses."

"Good, good! Now you look here, young man! You get Rowl to give you a drink and hang on until your father comes in, and we'll see if we can straighten out this crazy notion of yours."

But his father came in staggering under his load of euphorics, in no condition to talk sense. Snorting with annoyance the old man sent Rowl for antidotes and ice.

"Now you get your head clear, and fast!" he exclaimed. "When are you going to latch on to the fact that you have responsibilities, Derry? Here's this boy of yours full of some crackbrain plan to run away from Earth, and you're so piped you can barely walk!"

"He's what?" His father turned a bulbous glare on Horn. "He's got a plan to *what?*"

"That's better," the old man said sharply. "At least you're paying attention now. Well, boy, tell us the whole story and we'll see about it."

Horn complied. He hadn't intended to explain, but only to demand the money he needed and march out, leaving his relatives to ask one another what they had done to drive him away. Somehow, though, once he started talking he couldn't stop, and all kinds of things which he knew even before he mentioned them his listeners would not understand came tumbling out.

"So because your carnival week was spoiled by some off-planet character getting himself stuck with a knife," said his father at last, "you want to renege on all your family obligations and hide your head on some backward ball of mud like the one he probably came from!"

"Family obligations!" flared Horn. "That's good, coming from you! I never saw you do anything with family

62

obligations except off-load them on to Grandad's back! Do you know where your wife is right now?"

"Why, you foul-mouthed little—!" For an instant it looked as though his father was going to jump up and take a swing at him. Then his grandfather's curt voice broke in.

"Sit down, Derry. Control yourself. There's nothing wrong with the boy which a whipping would help, and anyhow he's too old to be treated that way by now. Or should be. If it hadn't been for this android at the hotel stuffing his ears with all kinds of nonsense about the man who got killed—"

"It isn't nonsense!" Horn stamped his foot.

"No, you must take it pretty seriously," his grand-father agreed sarcastically. "Asking a hundred thousand to help you run off and—and become a citizen of the galaxy or rescue a fair maiden from a man-eating tree or something equally absurd. But you can't expect anyone *else* to take it seriously."

"Well, hell, make it fifty thousand, enough for a one-way trip instead of a round one! Or—no, forget I asked for anything! I still have practically all my carnival allowance, and there must be a cheaper way of getting off Earth than shipping in a luxury liner!" Horn started for the door.

"Dad," said his father, plucking at the old man's sleeve. "Dad, I think he really means it."

"Yes, of course he does. Right this minute he means every word of it. But you know the next we'll hear of him if he does walk out, don't you? There'll be a signal from some benighted mudball out in the wide black yonder saying to send him his fare and he'll come home and be a good little boy again!"

"Come home? To what? A life as rigidly programmed as one of your robots—only they're lucky. *They* aren't designed with the capacity to resent it." Horn had to clench his fists to stop his hands from trembling.

A dangerous glint showed in his grandfather's eyes; he had never allowed anyone to voice criticism of his robots within the four walls of his home. Still he remained relatively calm, and spoke in a reasonable tone.

"Now, boy, think it through again, just to please me. I can well understand how the idea of this romantic knight-errantry must appeal to you, but do look at it in perspective. Remember you were told all this by an android—weren't you? And it's notorious that when they're under exceptional strain androids sometimes come up with the wildest notions, isn't it?"

"I'm beginning to wonder whether androids aren't better off than I am! At least when they're trained they're given a useful job of work to do, and that's more than I can ever look forward to if I stay here!"

There was an awful icy silence, during which Horn knew sickly that he had overstepped the limits of his grandfather's already tenuous patience. It was like waiting for the skies to fall.

"Very well," the old man said at last. "Very well. If that's how you feel about the advantages I've provided for you, I guess you had better leave Earth. And the sooner the better. Rowl! Have a heli brought out and program it for Faraway Field! Since you think androids do more useful work than I or your father, you young devil, I'm going to let you *do* an android's work for a while! There's a ship loading a consignment of robots on the field this minute—its from Newholme and its crew don't observe carnival. I was intending to ship an android as supercargo. I'll send you instead. Don't interrupt!" he thundered at his son, who was feebly protesting. "If you'd raised the kid better it would never have come to this! He's going to have to learn the hard way what decent folk think of fools who prefer androids to their own kith and kin!"

So angry he could barely speak, he pointed a quivering arm towards the door.

"Out!" he said thickly. "And *stay* out!"

CHAPTER IX

"HERE'S WHERE the supercargo bunks," said Dize, the brawny first mate of the interstellar freighter. He pointed through a door so narrow it was barely more than a hatchway. "Stow your duffle and get back to number one hold to check the cargo manifest. You got twenty-five minutes."

Obediently struggling with the one large bag his grandfather had permitted him to bring and finding it almost too large to squeeze through the opening, Horn complied. His face fell as he saw the cramped cabin he had been assigned.

"Don't look so sour!" Dize grunted. "Android quarters—what do you expect? And you got more room than on some ships I could name. We've had 'em in there head and shoulders taller than you, and glad of so much space to stretch out in! Okay—number one hold in twenty-five minutes from now."

His footsteps receded down the corridor. Horn dumped his bag on the bunk, sat down beside it and buried his face in his hands.

Well, that was that. For better or worse, he was on his own. At least he'd got what he'd asked for, and that was something of an achievement in itself. Few people could boast of having got something out of Grandfather Horn which he'd not at first been willing to concede. He clung to that slender consolation, lowered his hands and surveyed the cabin. It held the bunk he was sitting on—nearly as hard as the bench in Berl's heli; a locker containing a standard android poncho of coarse burlap and a pair of issue sandals much too small for him; a wash-bowl with a pressure tap aimed squarely at the open drain. And nothing.

Realizing with a start that five of his precious minutes had been lost in mooning, he set about stowing his gear as best he could. The locker was full almost at once, and he had to leave the bulk of what he'd brought in the case, which he contrived to slide underneath the bunk. He was still wearing a gaudy carnival rig because he'd taken nothing else away from home with him; he stripped it off and changed into more practical garb.

Over the washbowl there were a few square inches of mirror. Catching sight of himself, he noted that he ought to have a shave; black stubble was disfiguring his cheeks and chin. But in his haste he had picked up a jar of depilatory with only a smear left in the bottom, instead of the full one next to it. Annoyed at his mistake, he took a second look at himself and wondered whether he might try letting his beard grow. Sure, why not? He tossed the jar into the disposal chute.

Abruptly he remembered that he still had to find his way to the hold where Dize was expecting him, and had no idea even which end of the ship it was. He scrambled out of the cabin, stared down a maze of passages in which he shortly became hopelessly lost. It was more by luck than judgment that he ultimately reached the right place and found Dize fuming with impatience.

"Where the hell have you been, Horn? I can see this trip's going to be a rough one! Shipping with a human supercargo—whoever heard of anything so stupid? Androids at least do as they're told!"

Cheeks burning, Horn accepted the cargo manifest Dize thrust at him and began laboriously to check it.

Crate after crate of robots, lying passive in their plastic coffins, awaiting their personal dawn on Newholme. Incomprehensible identity codes which he had to ask to have explained to him; even when he'd got the hang of the markings he had trouble, because some of the crates had been stowed upside-down to make the most of the hold-space, and he had to clamber and crane and peer down gaps to find their codes. At the end he seemed to have several crates left over. With wordless contempt Dize showed where he had turned over two pages of the manifest at once.

"*All* right," he said at long last. "Back to quarters with you. Chow's in a quarter-hour, and we lift two hours after that. Don't know what we're doing about feeding you— guess we can't fill you up with android staple, seeing you're human. Anyway, I suppose you ought to show at the mess, be introduced to Captain Larrow. Think you can find your way?"

But when Horn diffidently slid back the door of the mess to discover Larrow already at table, he was met with a frosty glare and a bellow.

"Are you Horn? Well then, what in hell are you doing here?"

"I told him to come, captain," Dize said from the opposite end of the dining-table.

"Then you damned well shouldn't have. Old man Horn gave strict explicit orders that the boy was to be treated exactly like the regular kind of supercargo. In my book that means he eats android food—and I've half a mind to have him put on an android poncho, too, but I guess that rig he's in will be a bit more practical." He was a red-faced man with bristling eyebrows like a battery of miniature guns, and they waggled up and down as he spoke, raking Horn from head to foot. "Mr. Arglewain!"

"Sir?"—from another crewman sitting next to Dize.

"Go and issue him a measure of android staple. And get this, Horn! Mr. Arglewain's the steward. You're to report to him five minutes before every chow-time from now on and collect your rations, understood? If you're not prompt you don't eat. You probably won't care for the staple after your fancy diet on Earth, but it's what you'll be getting so you'd best learn to appreciate it. I've lived on it for days together myself, and it never did me any harm."

The android staple was a mushy grey-green goo—some kind of algae emulsified and fortified, Horn guessed.

67

Experimentally, although he was not in fact hungry, he choked a little of it down in the seclusion of his cabin. It came right back up again twenty minutes after the ship had lifted.

"You'll get over it," said Dize unsympathetically when he looked in an hour or so later. "In fact, you'll damned well have to get over it, and inside eight hours, at that. A supercargo is kept pretty busy aboard a tub like this. Well, catch some sleep if you can, and I'll rout you out at the beginning of your watch."

He turned to leave. Horn called feebly after him. "Say—just a moment, Mr. Dize!"

"What is it?"

"You're from Newholme, aren't you?"

"Of course. This is a Newholmer ship you're flying with."

"What's it like on Newholme? I mean, what's it *really* like?" Horn was struggling to sit up, his face almost the color of the undigested android staple he had thrown up.

"That's kind of a funny question," Dize said slowly. "Don't they teach galactography in Earthside schools?"

Horn made a vague gesture. "That's not what I want to know, the kind of thing they teach in schools. You can't find out about what interests me—whatever it is that marks off the people of one world from those of another. I don't mean the clothes they wear or the food they like to eat. I don't mean anything you can make lists or take solidos of. That's why I told my grandfather I wanted to get off Earth, because I suddenly needed to know things which no one could tell me back there."

"Is that the truth you're telling me—that you *wanted* to come off Earth? It wasn't just what I heard talk of, a row with your grandfather?" Dize cocked his head suspiciously.

"My asking for the money to leave Earth with was what started the row."

"Ah-hah," Dize nodded. "*I* get. Might have guessed, come to that. I never met your grandfather, but we

68

specialize in shipping his robots out for him, and I always pictured him as the kind of guy who thinks Earth is the whole of the universe."

"I promise you I'm not," Horn said weakly.

"All right, I believe you. But you look pretty sick right now. You stretch out and catch some sleep like I told you. Later on you'll have all the time in the galaxy to answer that question of yours."

After that, things weren't nearly as bad as he'd expected; Dize's affectation of gruffness gradually gave way to a sort of rough, rather patronizing, friendliness, and the process accelerated as he discovered that Horn was genuinely anxious not to be a nuisance and to do his best. Every now and then a trace of weary contempt for soft-handed Earthmen who were used to having everything done for them by machinery did still climax in a bout of vivid cursing, but this was invariably followed by a quick, economical and easily understood lesson in whatever technique Horn was finding troublesome, so that there was never a second recurrence of the same problem.

"Well, I can say this for you, Horn," he admitted grudgingly three days out from Earth. "You're not stupid. Just ignorant is all. And I guess you can't help that, can you?"

Horn felt himself flushing. Under Dize's guidance he was carrying out a check of the hull plates to make sure they were screening free-space radiation properly; heavy cosmics could play merry hell with the delicate electronic balance in a robot brain. He said, "Well—ah—this sort of job doesn't turn up too much on Earth these days."

"You mean you'd turn the whole thing over to automatics and just monitor them from a central instrument board?" Dize suggested.

"Yes, I guess that's what I'd have expected," Horn nodded.

"It's exactly what they do do aboard Earth's luxury

liners. And we could certainly do the same—after all, we build our own ships, and automatic radiation detectors are kids' stuff compared to interstellar engines. But I wouldn't like it. And there's the start of an answer to that question you put to me just after we lifted."

Horn looked briefly blank, then caught himself. "Oh! I was asking how Newholmers differed from—from Earth-siders, wasn't I?"

"Right." Dize perched on a handy crate and began to stuff a large foul-smelling pipe with some herbal mixture whose scent Horn had at first found pungent and irritating, but was growing adjusted to. "Why wouldn't we like it? Well, what would we do with our time during the trip?"

Horn recalled Dordy's sour remark about sitting in an android barracks and reading classics of literature. He nodded slowly.

"It's different aboard a liner," Dize said. "You can rely on any given bunch of passengers to keep the crew continually on the hop between takeoff and touchdown. A cargo of unactivated robots you'd just sit and stare at. You'd get bored. You'd get irritable. Me especially—I was born with a quick temper, as you've probably noticed."

Horn gave a wry grin.

"And what would you be doing right now? I mean if I wasn't chasing you to do hull-checks and air-monitoring and the rest of it? You'd be sitting on your backside in your cabin wondering if you'd been a complete idiot and what your chances were for signaling your grandfather to have the ship turned around and take you home. True?"

"You're damned right," Horn said. "It certainly stops me brooding."

"So there you are." Dize checked his watch. "Ah, almost chow-time. You can break off now."

And, ten minutes later, he reappeared at the door of Horn's cabin to find him spooning the drab staple into his mouth. "Come on!" he said, beckoning, and hurried him

70

down the corridor to the mess. Astonished, Horn hesitated in the entrance as Larrow looked up frostily.

But his next response was to gesture at an unoccupied place between Dize's and Arglewain's. "Join us, Mr. Horn," he invited. "Mr. Dize tells me he thinks you would be an asset to our company."

Three days further out they took the Big Step around the intervening light-years—the step which, for some reason no one understood, one ship in a million flights never completed—and began their braking run into the Newholme system. But Horn's own personal Big Step had already taken place.

When they had put down and cleared their holds, and he had had his first glimpse of another world (a disappointing one, for spaceports on every planet were much the same), he went back to his cabin and gathered his belongings prior to signing off the complement. Dize found him there testing a comb on the beard he had sprouted during the twelve days in space, which was already nearly long enough to look neat.

"Got something for you, Horn," he said. "Here!"

He held out a small envelope which Horn, puzzled, took and opened. Inside was a wad of what he instantly recognised as currency notes, though the design and color were unfamiliar and the bold lettering on each bill identified the issuing authority as the Planetary Republic of Newholme.

"What's this for?" he demanded.

"It's the going rate for the number of hours' work you put in," Dize grunted, seeming oddly embarrassed. "You see, we thought we ought to draw the line somewhere— about treating you like an android—and since your grandfather sort of kicked you off Earth without the polite goodbyes, well . . ."

"Oh, I'm not broke!" Horn exclaimed. "I still have the allowance he gave me for carnival week, and I guess Earthside currency can be changed easily enough."

He made to give it back, but Dize waved it aside, sitting

71

down on the bunk and lighting his pipe again.

"No, you earned it—you keep it. Larrow's a martinet, but he's dogmatic about his men having what they deserve. And—ah—speaking for myself, at least, any time you decide you want to work your passage back home, you just hang around this port until we show up, and you'll have got yourself the job you need."

Feeling absurdly flattered, Horn shrugged and slipped the Newholme money into his billfold. "By the way," he said, "I just realized! I never asked what you ship the other way—to Earth. You don't go back empty, presumably."

"No, of course not. We carry androids."

"*What*!" Horn was so startled he dropped his comb into the washbowl. "In the same holds as the robots?"

"Sure. Except the one we pick for supercargo. He gets to use this cabin. We fix up sort of collapsible bunks instead of the crate-racks, and they make out pretty well."

Horn stared at him for a long moment, then gave a forced laugh. "Remind me not to take up your offer of a working trip home, then," he said. "Crated robots sound a lot easier to handle."

"Oh, androids aren't troublesome. Can't be! They're conditioned out of it." Dize sucked on his pipe and emitted dense clouds of aromatic smoke.

Horn pondered for a while. "Hmmm! I guess you can fit a good few androids into those holds of yours, then. Funny! I always had this impression that most of the androids on Earth were made right there."

"Well, probably a good few of them are, but not by any means all. We ship eight hundred at a time, every thirty days or so. They don't come from Newholme, of course—they just transship 'em here. They're made further out. Lygos way, I believe, or Creew 'n Dith."

So the *cachet* of owning Rowl, an imported android, was all illusory! Horn almost laughed, then realized that perhaps thirty years ago this hadn't been the case. After all, it would make sense in view of the extremely high cost

72

of employing trained Earthside technicians to set up android factories on less expensive planets. The raw materials could be had cheaply on any Earth-like world.

There was a pause. Dize broke the silence with a cough. "Well, if you're planning to stay on Newholme for a while, I guess it's up to us to show you around. Like to ride into town with me and let me acquaint you with a few people?"

"That'd be great! Just let me check I have everything, then." Horn glanced into the locker and under the bunk, made sure his cash was safe in his pocket, and finally took out the little grey woven-metal wallet containing Talibrand's certificate, to reassure himself it really existed. He was about to pocket that also when Dize's hand closed on his wrist with an iron grip.

"What the hell are you doing with one of those?" the spaceman rasped. "*You* never did anything that could earn you this, you—you lousy Earthside imposter!"

CHAPTER X

TENSION FROZE THE AIR, like a crumb of ice dropped into supercooled water. Horn forced a nervous grin.

"Why not look inside?" he suggested. "It's not mine, and I'm not trying to pretend it is."

Suspiciously Dize drew out the booklet, opened it, and saw the greyness of the dead solido picture. He read the various certificates, thumbed through the pages and pages of exit and entry stamps, and finally returned his hard gaze to Horn's face.

"So how did you come by it? And what happened to the man it belonged to?"

"He was killed in the hotel I was staying at, the first night of carnival week. He'd given that to the manager's secretary—an android. And because I found the body, the

73

android gave it to me." Horn hesitated. "And . . . well, I guess I didn't tell you the whole truth about why I left Earth. I was just so sick of the—the pointlessness of my existence back there, that when I saw this certificate of Talibrand's I thought somebody ought to go back along the line he'd followed, and maybe bring the news of his death, and . . . oh, I don't know. I had this half-baked notion somebody ought to pick up his work where he left off."

"You?" Dize said.

"I . . ." Horn had to swallow very hard. "I seem to have been sort of elected. I mean, someone tried to kill me the next morning, simply because I'd taken too much interest in Talibrand's murder. At least I can't imagine any other reason."

"So what happened to this man who tried to kill you?"

"I killed him."

"Did you now?" Dize said thoughtfully.

"Oh, quite legally!" Horn hastened to assure him. "He challenged me to a duel without finding out beforehand that I'd won an award for my swordplay."

"Now there's another way in which we outworlders differ from you on Earth. We got enough risk in our daily lives without having to provide the artificial excitement of dueling to add a bit of spice. Newholme's a long-settled planet, but it's not nearly as—as *domesticated* as Earth is." He hesitated. "Are you serious about this, Horn?"

"I wish I knew," Horn confessed miserably. "You see, I'd never even heard of these 'citizens of the galaxy' before. I don't know what they do, I don't know what kind of people they are—except obviously that they're exceptional types. Look, you recognized this certificate the moment you set eyes on it! Had you seen one before?"

"Only in pictures." Dize closed the booklet, hesitated, returned it to its wallet and handed it back. "All right, I believe you. And I guess Earth can't be as bad as I always imagined, seeing a person like you can feel this strongly about someone from another planet. So what do you want o be told about the citizens of the galaxy?"

"Everything. What they do, who they are—everything!"

"What they do," Dize said musingly, "is more than the rest of us put together and slightly better. Who they are—well, I can tell you about a couple of them, I guess. Right now there are three altogether. Correction: two, if Lars Talibrand is dead. So that was his name, was it? Talibrand! Sorry, that must sound pretty strange to you. You see, we heard a few years ago that another citizen of the galaxy had been nominated, but his identity was never published, because they said if the word got around it would handicap whatever he was doing. So the honor can't have been of much practical use to him. Damnation! This is bad news, Horn—you've no idea just *how* bad!"

"But as for the others ... Well, Gayk on Vernier is a biologist. He synthesized some kind of bacteriophage which he claimed would deal with half a dozen diseases nobody had ever managed to cure before. He infected himself with all of them at once—refused to try it on volunteers in case it didn't work."

"And it did?"

"Sure. But it was himself he tried it on first."

"He sounds like a brave man," Horn said inanely. "How about the other one?"

"A spaceman from Arthworld, called Yugus. There was a star due to go nova out that way. They'd never managed to monitor the full spectroscopic output of a nova before. They planted a whole townful of equipment on its inmost planet to signal back data. Turned out the noise from the star was making nonsense of the information. But they wanted the records pretty bad. So Yugus came up with a crazy scheme to go in and get them and let the radiation-pressure from the actual explosion blow him away. And he managed it. He was crippled for four-five years afterwards, but because of what he did every inhabited planet can monitor its primary and be sure that it's not going to nova without warning and burn them to a crisp.

Which fitted the qualification for galactic citizenship."

"That being—?"

"You have to do something which benefits the entire population of more than one planet."

That almost made Horn feel giddy. It was a long while before he could ask, "And you don't know about Talibrand's work, you say?"

"Nope." Dize shrugged. "There are lots of rumors, naturally. Some people say he stumbled across a medical blackmail ring—that's when someone gets a corner on the cure for an endemic disease, and hoists the price knowing that sick people will pay anything, or waters the drug down so they'll go on being sick instead of recovering completely."

"Would they hate him so much they'd hunt him clear to Earth and have him killed?"

"It's possible. I guess now he's dead they may announce what he was up to. Or maybe they won't, because he didn't finish the job and would have wanted someone to take over." Dize hesitated. "Well, what's your reaction to what I've been telling you?"

"I'm scared," Horn said abruptly. "But . . ."

"But what?"

"But someone who could earn one of these"—he hefted the certificate in its wallet—"deserves to have someone fit for the job take over for him. And the place they're likeliest to know about who that person is I imagine must be the world he himself hailed from: Creew'n Dith. So I'll see if I can make my way there."

"You only need to walk into the government office right here on Newholme, show that certificate and say you discovered Talibrand's body, and you'll be given a free flight there on a luxury liner."

Horn thought that over, and finally shook his head. "I guess maybe it would be better if I didn't," he said. "It'd attract new coverage and all sorts of publicity. No, if I have to I can probably pay my way. Or work my passage."

Dize tapped out his pipe on the washbowl and rinsed away the dottle. "I like the way you think, Horn," he said, and there was no trace of his former patronizing tone. "Come on—let's take a ride into town and find ourselves a drink."

Now the sensation of being elsewhere than on Earth really started to assail him. Superficialities, first: the different materials used to pave the roads, the different layout of the houses, smaller but not so closely packed together. There were hardly any private helis—though big public hundred-seater models lined the edge of the spaceport. Most of the traffic consisted of groundcars that hummed and crackled as they passed, running, so Dize told him, on solar conversion batteries at present because it was local summer, but in winter using broadcast power.

After the differences, the identities. The streets of the town they traveled to, aboard a public groundcar seating sixty which they caught at the exit from the spaceport were lined with men and women of the same species as on Earth—their clothing strange, their average complexion significantly paler because so much more emigration had taken place from rich countries than poor ones during the great phase of human colonisation, and perhaps half a head shorter on average than their Earthside cousins. But still they were human beings.

Poorer human beings. That was a point. Their bus was controlled by a human driver; on Earth, of course, all public transport no matter how short the distance it operated over was in the care of unwearying automatics. It struck Horn that a reliable index of living standard must be the number of repetitive tasks still assigned to human beings.

Surely, though, merely plying a bus back and fourth over a fixed route was something an android could have done just as well as a man, without wasting the man's special talents? He mentioned this point to Dize, who gave a dry laugh.

"How many androids have you seen since you landed?"

Horn hesitated. "Well—ah . . ."

"Any at all? Thought not? Man, androids *cost!* You can go weeks at a time on Newholme, even in a big city, and not see one of them. Ninety per cent of the androids here at any given moment are in transit to Earth. We pass 'em on, and in exchange we get robots. Androids we can manage without, robots not."

"Don't you build robots on Newholme?"

"Sure, but they're not in the same class with the ones your grandad makes."

"Even so, running a bus—"

"Watch the driver for a while. He knows his regular passengers, doesn't he? Chats with them friendly! We like that, here on Newholme. Oh, sure we're going to go automatic eventually, but right now we're still scraping the surface of our planetary resources. We need the advanced robots we can build or buy for the dangerous jobs where you wouldn't risk a human life—mining, working under the oceans, clearing the straits between islands of the rocks which get in the way of our submarines. Get the picture? Ah, here we are—this is my stop!"

Obediently Horn followed him to the exit, and found himself in a quiet residential street with native trees shading long one-storey houses. Dize flung open the gate of the nearest and two boys of about eight and ten came clamoring to greet him.

Horn hung back in slight embarrassment. He hadn't realized that Dize proposed to take him home. But, picking up one of his sons on each arm, the spaceman called for him to come on in. At the door they were met by a pretty little woman with long fair hair of a shade seldom seen on Earth nowadays unless it was dyed, and Dize introduced her as his wife Maj-Brith.

"This is Derry Horn," he added. "Shipped with us this trip. He's from Earth, but he's all right."

That was a backhanded compliment, Horn thought, but

he controlled his reaction and smilingly shook his hostess's hand.

For a while thereafter, as Dize reported to his sons on the trip just past, he was left by himself at the side of a large living-room full of solid furniture in native woods and what he took to be real animal hide. Maj-Brith brought big pottery mugs containing a dark drink—a local beer, Horn judged—which he tasted and found rather sour. He sat cradling the mug in both hands and mentally comparing the decor with the lightness and insubstantiality of a typical Earthly home.

At length Dize told the boys to run along and turned to his guest.

"Sorry about that, but unless I get my trip-report over with there's no peace in the house! Well, anyhow, there was something I guess maybe I should have warned you about before now, but it's not too late. Reason I brought you home with me, in fact."

He leaned forward, holding out his mug for Maj-Brith to refill.

"Look, if you just start marching around Newholme, or any other of the outworlds, you're going to attract attention like a fire-heli or a parade band! I don't care how quickly that beard of yours grows—it's not going to disguise the fact that you're from Earth. So you go buy a suit of Newholmer clothes: that doesn't fix it either, because every time you open your mouth either your accent or what you say will mark you out. If I'm to believe what you told me just before we quit the ship, someone tried to have you killed. That kind of someone won't be put off very easily. Am I right?"

"I would expect him to be pretty persistent," Horn agreed. His voice was calm and level, but deep inside he was very frightened at the thought of what he had committed himself to do.

"So okay," Dize continued. "I've been doing some thinking. I assume this 'someone' has been, too. Now if he learned that young Derry Horn, of the family of Horn &

Horn Robots, had gone off Earth so quickly after being involved in the aftermath of Talibrand's murder, would he also hear about your row with your grandad?"

Horn shook his head. "We like to keep our—ah—family differences private."

"Right. So if he discovered you'd come to Newholme, he'd go checking luxury hotels and resorts, sounding out the agents who represent Horn & Horn products here, and all like that. It might take him a few days to realize you weren't in any of the proper places. You'd damned well better not be, then! In fact, you'd better stay here—no, don't interrupt!" He raised a broad palm to forestall objections. "I got a few day's layover to waste before we load our next cargo. And you learn pretty quick; I've seen that for myself. I can't turn you into any specific kind of outworlder, but I can at least show you the things that set you off particularly as an Earthman, which is the rarest of all kinds of foreigner on every single other planet. Meanwhile, I'll check at the port and see when there's a convenient ship bound for Creew 'n Dith. Since that's the planet which issued Talibrand's certificate in the first place, I can't imagine anywhere that you'd be safer."

He brushed aside Horn's profuse thanks, holding out his mug for yet another refill, and begin to stuff his pipe.

"All the thanks I need is for you to stick at what you've started," he said. "I don't have the faintest idea what it is, but if a citizen of the galaxy was involved, it absolutely *has* to be important."

CHAPTER XI

HORN FELT LIKE the hero of one of the fairy-tales he remembered from his childhood, who had come into possession of a charm that opened any door. He had foreseen all sorts of difficulties when he tried to cope on his own after reaching Newholme. Thanks to Talibrand's certificate and Dize's generosity, he found himself being helped at every turn and warned of problems he had never suspected might exist.

Studying the certificate, he noticed something he had previously overlooked, which meant that a long stay on Newholme would be a waste of time under any circumstances even if he had not already decided to move on to Crew 'n Dith as soon as possible. Newholme was unique—apart from Earth, of course—among the many worlds which Talibrand had visited: he had been to it only once. It followed logically that his regular business, whatever that was, had never brought him this way. His most frequent calls had been made on his home planet, on Vernier, Lygos and Arthworld.

What could he have been on the trail of? Well, perhaps the answer could be found on Crew 'n Dith.

According to a map of the occupied galaxy which he borrowed from Dize, that was the world just beyond the regular liner routes. If he had wanted to go to a nearer system, he could have done so on comparatively luxurious vessels; there were plenty of travelers to support scheduled passenger services, mainly sales representatives and import-export agents, plus a few exceptionally wealthy tourists and a trickle of diplomats and other officials.

But when Dize had finished his check at the spaceport, he returned home to report that the only ship going straight from here to Crew 'n Dith in the next month or more was a freighter carrying another consignment of robots, a good few of which were actually products of Horn & Horn. There was no other flight scheduled that route at all.

"Hmmm!" Horn combed his new beard with his fingers, cogitating over the map. He had just been struck by the fact that there was a fringe of uncertainty fifty or sixty systems off, where the names of worlds were spelled

81

phonetically and followed by a query, or entered in brackets against more than one star because it was not known exactly which they circled. That, more than anything else, brought it home to him that when human beings referred to "the galaxy" they were actually talking about a very small portion of it comparatively close to Earth.

"This freighter carrying robots to Creew 'n Dith, now," he mused aloud. "Would it also be bringing androids in the opposite direction?"

"Very likely," Dize shrugged. "You can fit three androids in the space you need for eight crated robots, which must about correspond to their relative costs, because that's the way it's been since before I entered the space service. Economically it's a hell of a stable trade, and a good one for the people who work in it."

Horn raised his eyes from contemplation of the map, and whistled. In that case Rowl, the *imported* android, must already have been one among many when he was bought by the Horn family. If Larrow's ship alone was delivering nearly ten thousand annually over the last leg of their voyage to Earth, androids from the outworlds must be absolutely pouring in!

"Well, that suggests an explanation for Talibrand confiding his precious certificate to an android, I guess," he said at length. "If Dordy was imported, maybe he'd learned on his way to Earth how important a galactic citizen's work was, whereas hardly anyone else on the planet would have heard of such people. Interesting! But never mind that."

He leaned forward. "Now you said this ship bound for Creew 'n Dith was carrying some of our robots?"

"A fair slice of the cargo we ourselves brought out last trip," Dize nodded. "Plus a bunch of others made here on Newholme."

"Cheaper?"

"Sure, a lot cheaper."

"And from what you've told me about Creewndithians"—Horn had had a number of long talks with Dize about the people of the various outworlds since his arrival here—"I don't imagine they'd cooperate by agreeing to let me work a passage with them."

Dize chuckled. "Not in a million years!"

"So I guess I'd better come out from behind my anonymity and start exploiting grandad's dislike of letting our family rows be noised around. As far as anyone here can tell, it would be perfectly reasonable for a scion of Horn & Horn Robots to make a tour of the worlds that imported our products and get firsthand knowledge of the uses they're put to. We'll go down to the port tomorrow and set it up."

Dressed in the height of Earthly fashion, affecting a lazy disinterest which matched his ostensible role of a grandson and heir apparent rather unwillingly learning the family business, he lounged examining his fingernails in the office of the agency which had chartered the Creewndithian ship due to leave the following day, while various alternative proposals were put to him.

Go via some other nearer system, so that you need only transship at the last moment from a nice comfortable passenger liner?

"No," Horn said firmly. "That would involve delay. I'd rather spend the least possible time away from Earth. *I* don't mind shipping on a cargo tub if I can get there and back a good deal quicker."

Wait for the biennial visit of the *Regulus*, which was available for diversion to Creew 'n Dith on payment of a surcharge which no doubt the resources of Horn & Horn could meet without noticing?

"I said I want to get there quickly!" Horn said, betraying a hint of annoyance.

And so on, and so on, until finally they parted with the information that there was, actually, a freighter under a certain Captain Shembo, scheduled to lift tomorrow on the direct route, which ordinarily didn't accept passengers but which in view of the exceptional circumstances . . .

"Ask how much they want," Horn said boredly, and gave the gap-toothed woman in charge of the office a sight of a thick wad of Earthside currency he was carrying. She beamed and went into action as though afraid the money might evaporate if left exposed to the air.

"Yes, sir! I'll attend to your comfort aboard the ship myself. I'll have the captain's cabin put at your disposal—"

"You must be out of your mind," Horn cut in. "It'll put the captain in a filthy temper, and he's liable to take it out on his crew. I'd prefer my trip to be made in a more pleasant atmosphere. Turn out one of the second mates, perhaps." He gave the gap-toothed woman a sunny smile. "When my grandfather, the president of Horn & Horn, gets a touch of dyspepsia, production suffers for two days following. I've seen it happen."

The remark was something of a libel on his grandfather, but it had the desired effect, and he left the woman bubbling with her impression of his charm, good sense and breeding.

Considering it was such a long flight, the fare he'd been asked was lower than he'd imagined. As Dize had explained to him, the purchasing power of Earthside money went up, broadly speaking, in ratio to the distance from Earth, although naturally the available range of goods you could buy with it grew rapidly smaller. So he had no compunction about spending the rest of his Newholmer money on a sight-seeing trip for the Dize family; it seemed like a good way to mark his—and incidentally also Dize's own—impending departure.

Next morning he and Dize went to the spaceport together. Larrow's ship was due to lift at sunset, but Dize had to be on hand early to supervise the loading of their android cargo.

This, they discovered, was already on the port. A light drizzle was falling from the overcast sky and a chilly wind was blowing. In a compound adjacent to the freight warehouses, hundreds of blue-skinned men stood or sat huddled together, with only their issue ponchos for protection. Dize clapped his hands to his forehead in dismay.

"Damn these fools of port officials!" he exclaimed. "Why haven't they rigged the awning yet? We're liable to have half the batch go down with pneumonia if they're put aboard soaking wet! Excuse me—I'm going to raise some hell."

He vanished with a vague promise to come back and see Horn off, and the latter, with many backward glances at the miserable androids, made his way slowly to the port authority office.

Here Captain Shembo was waiting to greet him: a wiry man with disproportionately long arms who spoke thickly and with many hesitations. This at first irritated Horn, by making him feel he was dealing with a person of subnormal intelligence; abruptly he realized that a starship commander couldn't *be* that stupid, and remembered that, being Creewndithian, Shembo was struggling with a foreign language. The reality of any mode of communication other than the Anglic Terrestrial to which he had been born had never penetrated Horn's awareness before. He made up his mind to pick up at least a snatch of Creewndithian during the trip.

It rapidly became clear that Shembo was anxious to be on good terms with his unexpected but important passenger, and when the formalities of port control were over he undertook to escort him personally to the ship. Doubtless this was intended as a compliment; however—perhaps, Horn guessed, because such conveniences were rare on Creew 'n Dith—it didn't seem to occur to the captain to signal for a groundcar, and they trudged together across the concrete of the landing-ground under a bombardment of icy drizzle.

By now, Dize's complaints had paid dividends, and the androids were struggling to erect big awnings on poles, which flapped like the wings of a dying bird. Seeing the direction of his companion's gaze, Shembo gave a wide smile.

"Good cargo, huh? We brung in many this trip!"

"That's the bunch you just brought in? They're from Creew 'n Dith, then?"

"Oh no! Androids come from far out. Long far. Maybe twice as far—I not know. We get from other ships on Creew 'n Dith four cargoes. I buy best of each at—at ... How do you say what is, when each makes his biggest price?"

"Auction?" Horn suggested after a moment's reflection. Shembo ringed his thumb and forefinger in a gesture of agreement.

"Oction, is right. I very good buyer for androids, I get best ones and treat well. Lose few lives! Other traders not so good, pay low prices, get bad stock, give bad food, not keep warm, lose many, try get more price than worth after. Best do business with *good* androids."

So these androids came from even further out than Creew 'n Dith, did they? Horn raised his eyebrows in surprise. Offhand he would have been inclined to doubt that anywhere less advanced than, say, Newholme could support the complex technology of artificial life manufacture. Why, though, should he assume it was all that complicated? Once you'd programmed your basic germ plasm correctly, and set up whatever kind of womb-surrogate you needed to nourish the developing embryo, you could no doubt reduce the process to a series of rote tasks. The raw materials were plentiful enough, that was certain. And once the infants had been decanted, or whatever the technical term was, doubtless they could be raised in pretty much the same fashion as human children until they were old enough for conditioning and training. Indeed, it might make very good sense for a remote and underdeveloped outworld to invest in an android plant, knowing that this above all was a product in demand on Earth and exchangeable for otherwise prohibitively expensive robots.

He had just been distracted from that line of thought by Shembo's proud indication of his ship, lying third in line of those waiting at the loading-berths, when a sharp voice hailed them from behind. They turned to discover one of the silent Newholmer groundcars, occupied by a driver and a passenger, both men; the latter was stepping down as the car halted.

"Mr. Horn? Sorry to trouble you," he said affably. "Could you come back to the port authority office for a moment? We overlooked a document you were supposed to sign—a pure formality, of course. You have to give an undertaking that you don't intend to set up permanently in business on Creew 'n Dith."

He added a faintly weary shrug, as though to imply. "You know what these regulations are like!"

Horn cursed silently, but aloud said only, "Sorry, Captain Shembo. I guess I'll have to do as he says. I'll get back as quickly as I can."

He took a pace forward, and was instantly dragged back. Astonished, he realized that Shembo had clamped one powerful hand on his arm, and with the other had conjured an ugly but efficient-looking projectile weapon from the folds of his uniform tunic.

"You not going anywhere, Mr. Horn!" he said between clenched teeth. "Is no such certificate for visitors to Creew 'n Dith! I guess maybe you very rich man. I guess these"—a word Horn didn't catch, presumably a Creewndithian obscenity—"try kidnap you for ransom. You get into ship. You *run!*"

87

CHAPTER XII

SUCH WAS THE TONE of authority Shembo used that—even though his mind was frozen with shock—Horn found his feet beginning to obey the order to head for the ship. He checked himself the moment he could think clearly again.

Kidnapping for ransom? That was something out of a historical melodrama! And yet the idea must be a very real one to Shembo for him to act so promptly upon it. Maybe among the outworlds such things did still go on. . . .

But he couldn't believe that it was so simple. Far more likely, in his view, was the alternative explanation. Yesterday he had emerged from anonymity when he went to book his passage aboard Shembo's ship. If Dize's guess was the right one, then the "someone" who had disposed of Lars Talibrand might very well have taken notice of his presence on Newholme.

He drew a deep breath. "Thank you very much, Captain Shembo! But I don't believe they want to kidnap me. I think it's far more likely that they want me killed!"

Hearing himself say that, knowing that it was true even though he was mainly uttering the words for effect, sent a shiver down his spine, but he managed to keep his eyes on the faces of the two men in the groundcar, and was pleased and dismayed at the same time to see their expressions of alarm.

"You serious, Mr. Horn?" Shembo demanded, aghast. But he kept both gaze and gun trained on the two strangers.

"Somebody's already tried it once, back home on Earth."

"In that case I guess maybe we call lawforce pretty

damn quick! You go to ship—"

"It was a lawforce superintendent who tried to kill me," Horn cut in.

"Hey! Things *really* bad down there on Earth now! So best they come to the ship, huh? My crew is good fellows. Soon beat plenty of truth out of 'em!"

He beckoned with the muzzle of his gun. "You! Come on out that car! You come get your feet wet same like us!"

For a moment Horn thought the strangers were about to comply. Then, suddenly and simultaneously, each of them made a curious sideways movement of the jaw, and keeled over: the passenger against the side of the car, the driver with his head on the windshield.

"Poison?" Shembo breathed. "Or faking?" He advanced cautiously, touched the arm of the passenger; when there was no reaction, he felt down the forearm for a pulse. After a moment he straightened and put away his gun.

"Is dead the both of them," he said in somber tones.

"Dead!" Horn darted forward. "Are you sure?"

"Certain sure, Mr. Horn. So all we can get out of them is maybe who they are." With brisk and practiced movements he rifled the pockets of both men, discovering wallets which he handed over to Horn. Accepting them in bewilderment, the latter started to voice a question.

"You talk later, Mr. Horn!" Shembo ordered. "Right now you come fast to ship. We lift right away, earlier than regular time! Put lots of distance behind you!"

"Behind me? But—"

"You talk later," Shembo repeated. "Mr. Dize, he told me you carry certificate of Lars Talibrand, citizen of galaxy! You not want to be delayed by arguments with lawforce, hm? So *move!*"

An hour later, in Shembo's own cabin—its walls, floor and ceiling shivering to the continual hammer-hammer of the interstellar engines, which were less well maintained than those of Larrow's ship, or perhaps just less well designed to avoid wasting power on surplus noise and vibration—the captain poured two tots from a bottle of some strong-smelling and fiery liquor. Raising his own glass, he favoured Horn with a mirthless grin.

"Sorry, Mr. Horn! When Dize first tell me you have Talibrand certificate, I say, 'Watch out! Is many first-rate tricksters come up from Earth!' Not till I see for self is someone trying to kidnap you can I believe what Dize say to me!" He tossed back his drink and reached for a refill.

Horn imitated the gesture, choked, spluttered and felt his eyes filling with tears. Shembo chuckled.

"Sorry again! Is good strong Creewndithian brandy—maybe you like better with little juice, hm?"

"No, never mind," Horn forced out, recovering. "Ah . . . I didn't realize you knew Dize!"

"Oh, sure. I do business many years with Captain Larrow and his crew. I bring androids, take away robots; they bring robots, take away androids. Is commercial acquaintance, yes? Not much friendly, but hello how are you sort of thing. So when he tell me is you who discovered dead body of Talibrand, I do like he asked me. *Hael!*" A second shot of the brandy went to join the first one.

Wiping his lips with the back of his hand, he went on, "And did be useful to you the wallets of the two men?"

"Yes and no," Horn said, producing them and laying them on the table between them. Drawing out the contents, which he had already inspected, he added in a low tone, "I get the feeling I'm carrying a plague! Until the other night on Earth, the first night of carnival, I'd never seen a dead body except once when someone was being carried out of a dueling-hall. And now they seem to be dropping dead all around me!"

"Is shame," Shembo declared. "Is too few people and too big galaxy for wasted deaths like that!"

"What—what did they die of, those two at the spaceport? Do you know?"

"Oh, sure!" Shembo looked surprised. "Poison in tooth—bite down and break hidden . . ." He snapped his

90

ingers. "Captule? Cap-*sule!* Is very old trick, use enturies ago."

"So someone is very anxious indeed to keep something secret," Horn muttered. "It must take expensive onditioning to make your agents willing to kill themelves when they're unmasked."

"Oh, sure! But people in business where they need to kill citizen of galaxy sure are very bad and very rich. Who vas they, the two who dead?"

"Well, according to the ID they were carrying, their names were Hyam Udd and Pedro Cavelgrune, and they vere both export-import agents from Maxplan. That's not far from Newholme, is it?"

"No. I was there two-three times. Is not good world for numans. Is too hot. Not much goods to trade. Like steambath and mudpack!"

"So export-import agents can't have their business illing their entire working time, hm? Apparently they specialized as agents for android cargoes, anyway. There are letters here in Cavelgrune's wallet which mention two or three consignments, and instruct him to employ the usual procedure'. But it doesn't say who sent them, I'm afraid."

"Anything else?" Shembo peered into one of the empty vallets.

"Nothing that makes sense to me," Horn muttered.

"Is something!" Shembo declared. He raised the wallet o his ear and bent it back and forth. "Is something stiff in here—is heavy paper, maybe. We look again, hm?" He produced a wicked-looking knife and prised apart the edge of the wallet, revealing a concealed compartment. From it he delicately withdrew another letter.

"I read Anglic handwriting pretty slow," he said, and handed it to Horn.

"We learn that a boy called—" Horn began aloud, and had to check and look again before continuing. "A boy called Derry Horn claiming to be the grandson of Horn he robot manufacturer intends to leave Newholme

aboard a Creewndithian ship at 1200 on 4/4/008. Since the
Creewndithian problem would have been solved on Earth
without trouble but for the interference of a person of the
same name, he is to be taken in charge, evaluated and if
necessary"—his voice cracked on the last word—
"eliminated!"

"Now," Shembo said solemnly, "I *really* believe what
Dize tell me!"

Horn stared at the letter in horror. The signature was
simply "Kyer," and there was no address but the
scribbled name of the city on Newholme which they had
just lifted from.

"You very pale, Mr. Horn," Shembo said with
sympathy. "You drink little more brandy, you soon feel
okay."

Horn complied, and somewhat to his surprise found the
potent liquor calming him, as Shembo had promised. For
a long while he sat in silence, cogitating.

What link was there between Coolin on Earth and
Cavelgrune on Newholme? What link, in fact—apart
from Talibrand's own travels—was there between all
these various outworlds and Horn's own narrow escape on
Earth? Only one factor kept recurring and recurring.

Androids.

Talibrand had confided his certificate to an android.
That same android had been an acute enough judge of
character to guess that Horn might be prodded into
leaving Earth on Talibrand's trail—something androids
were barred by law from doing, though having met Dordy
Horn could hardly doubt they were capable of doing it.
And now, once more, androids were the speciality of Udo
and Cavelgrune's export-import agency. It was the *only*
common factor!

He had a momentary vision of some vast android
organization spanning the stars, passing information by a
subterranean channel few humans ever guessed at, for use
in blackmail. Could that be it, a huge interstellar criminal
confederacy? Could that be the thing Lars Talibrand had

92

stumbled on? Dordy had pointed out that no android could be better off than any human, even one of the Dispossessed. Could he there have been voicing a jealousy which might lead to the passing on of rumor, scandal, slanderous lies—anything to make androids feel in some vague fashion superior to humans?

No, it didn't fit. It was ridiculous. He had to believe Dordy's assertion that Talibrand had voluntarily confided his certificate to him. If he had stolen it, he would never have handed it on to another human being and risked punishment for what he had done.

Waiting for him to finish thinking, Shembo had struck a smokehale and vanished into the first dense cloud of its vapor. He spoke out of the middle of it.

"You not what I think, Mr. Horn! When Dize tell me, I think first, 'Oh, I carry spoiled rich boy! I carry some big fool who make nuisance all time and complain, complain because my ship is not luxury liner!' Is good to find young man from Earth who not caves in like burst balloon when someone tries kill him!"

"If you could only read my mind . . ." Horn said wryly and tucked the incredible letter ordering his death back into the concealed compartment of the late Pedro Cavelgrune's wallet.

Shembo exposed all his shiny teeth in a grin of comprehension and disappeared again in a cloud of smoke.

"Sure, is sensible! Is more worth keeping life of person who not want kill other people than keep life of person who *does* want kill other people! So you get little bit scared, hm? Never you mind, Mr. Horn! Is safe here on this ship of mine! Is all good reliable crew, work with me long time."

"In the android trade," Horn muttered to himself. "Captain, I guess I ought to ask you something about this business you're in. I know practically nothing about it. I remember when I was a kid—oh, twelve or fourteen years ago—my grandfather was talking about buying himself a piece of it, as a diversification of his robot interests. But I don't recall anything coming of it."

Shembo chuckled. "He not manage to buy in," he said flatly.

"I guess he didn't. But how can you be so positive?"

The captain extended a hand with two fingers folded, two crossed. "Android trade tight like *that*," he said. "All so tight it not leak liquid helium!"

So it was a monopoly, and jealously guarded. Okay, if someone had had the bright idea of transporting an entire android factory to an underdeveloped outworld where his raw materials cost him literally nothing, he might be expected to want to hold on to his advantage as long as possible. Fair enough. Monopoly-breaking was hardly the kind of job to attract Lars Talibrand, was it? It was more the business of regular government authorities. Anyway, as for benefiting entire planetary populations, Dize had indicated that Earth was the chief consumer of androids, and Earth didn't recognize citizens of the galaxy.

"Do you have many androids on Creew 'n Dith, Captain Shembo?" he demanded.

"Few. Go to big houses, rich families. Sometimes when rich man drop by at port, he bid in oction to get specially good one. But not many, no."

"You have more use for robots, hm?"

"Sure. Androids pretty much same as people except not so onery. Robots good and useful—very strong, but tame!"

"So your cargo will all be bought up on Creew 'n Dith?"

"All? No, not all—is not very rich world, mine. Beautiful, exciting, yes, but not so rich. So sell some to dealers from further out, exchange for more androids."

Horn's brow corrugated with concentration. "Between Earth and Newholme the ratio seems to be eight robots to three androids. Is that the same on this leg of the route?"

"Hell, no! For eight robots I get six, maybe so many as ten androids when I sell on Creew 'n Dith! Robots worth more androids further you get from Earth, see? Earthside

94

robots the very best, Newholmer nearly so good, what we make on Creew 'n Dith not much worth exporting, see?''

That sounded reasonable, Horn decided. If the bulk of the androids traveling by the route to Earth originated out Arthworld way, or even perhaps somewhere still further from the solar system, this variation in their price was perfectly logical. Doubtless the losses Dize had referred to when he saw his next cargo exposed to the rain and wind—from pneumonia and similar causes—also affected their value, as must transportation costs . . .

Shembo had gone off into a highly technical account of price fluctuations in the android trade, which his command of Anglic was not really adequate for. Horn listened with only half an ear. After all, he might have come to an entirely false conclusion, and his next stop was the place where he was likeliest to be told about Talibrand's secret, by the authorities who had nominated him for galactic citizenship. He ought to stop guessing from flimsy evidence and wait until he was given something concrete to act upon.

CHAPTER XIII

"No, I WILL NOT tell you our reason for nominating Talibrand to this honor," said Hereditary Councillor Braithwin coldly. "But before you leave this hall I shall require to know *your* reason for asking such a stupid question!"

He was a man of medium height and great girth, with an aggressive lower lip and full rubicund cheeks. He sat in a throne-like chair of black and yellow native woods, padded with what looked like unprocessed animal furs, and he wore a black tunic and full black breeches with a gold-plated belt and soft leather calf-high boots. His Anglic was virtually perfect, displaying hardly a trace of the thick accent that obscured Shembo's speech.

95

Horn felt himself flushing under the accusing stare of the hereditary councillor. He was totally at a loss. He had been feeling like that ever since his arrival on Creew 'n Dith. Newholme, for all its superficial differences, might as well have been a regional backwater of Earth. But this!

He struggled to maintain his composure as he glanced around the hall, noting the women in long soft white dresses, many of them pretty, the men all in variants of the costume worn by Braithwin and somehow seeming more masculine than he was in his fashionable Earthside clothing; the low ceiling with its exposed timber beams, the walls of dressed stone with narrow windows climaxing in a point as abrupt as an arrowhead's, the succession of furs spread out on the tiled floor between the entrance and the spot where he stood facing Braithwin.

Mustering all his courage, he raised his voice to make certain everyone in the long hall heard him, looked the councillor straight in the eye, and demanded, "Is it not important to know for what reason a citizen of the galaxy was *killed*?"

"What?" Braithwin seized the arms of his chair and pulled his body forward from the waist, glaring at Horn. At the same moment a rustling cry of dismay ran through the assembly, followed by a buzz of talk as those who spoke Anglic translated for those who did not, and another outburst of cries which Braithwin silenced with a glare.

"Killed?" he rasped. "Lars Talibrand killed? Proof, I say!"

"I came from Earth to Newholme because Talibrand went from Newholme to Earth," Horn answered deliberately. "From Newholme I came to Creew 'n Dith because Talibrand went from Creew 'n Dith to Newholme. I know because I have—this!"

He whipped out Talibrand's certificate, held it up for everyone to see, and tossed it into Braithwin's lap.

"And carrying it," he finished, "I have been kept kicking my heels at your door because you would not admit me to an audience!"

Braithwin's burning eyes fixed him for a long moment. Then he uttered a curt sentence in Creewindithian. Horn had picked up enough odd words from Shembo during his voyage from Newholme to realize that it constituted a relatively polite order to the crowd to get the hell out, and he waited until he was alone with the councillor in the great echoing hall.

"You're no more'n a boy," Braithwin said at last, tapping the wallet on the back of his hand. "Spite of that beard you wear."

Horn didn't attempt to dispute the remark. The older man got to his feet and descended the steps of the dais from which he had presided over the assembly. He fell to absentminded pacing on the bare tiles, five steps one way, five another.

"So he's dead," he muttered almost inaudibly. "Rest him well. . . . But you, Horn! You have only yourself to blame for being kept kicking your heels at my door, haven't you? *You* put it about that you'd come to pry into the use we make of the robots we buy from Earth. I've got more important things to do with my time than answer a lot of empty-headed questions! This world's a sight different from yours, you know. Yours practically runs itself, I hear, what with your machines, your robots and androids and all. Here *we* look after the planet—we humans! We don't leave everything up to cogs and circuits and blue-skinned artificial men!"

He swung to face Horn directly, thrusting out the hand which held Talibrand's wallet so that one corner pointed at the younger man's heart. "Why the blazes didn't you say what you'd really come here for?"

"Because Talibrand was killed!" Horn flared. "Because whoever he was up against was able to try and have me killed in a duel on Earth, and later kidnap me on Newholme! Because Talibrand died with his work unfinished! What ought I to have done when I learned I'd got here ahead of the news from Earth—go out and shout

97

from the rooftops?''

Braithwin drew his beetling brows together and studied Horn thoughtfully for a long while. Abruptly he said, ''Let's get out of this drafty hall. I've held a long enough audience for today, anyhow. Come into my study and sit down.''

He pushed open a heavy wooden door behind the dais and led Horn into a small room with the same stone walls as the main hall, furnished with a rough wooden trestle table and half a dozen canvas-seated chairs. There were books, many of them from Earth, on shelves attached to the wall by pegs. A bellow materialized a brown-haired girl in the universal floor-length white dress, who carried a pottery jug and some mugs on a tray.

''Sit down and try the drink that's made us what we are,'' Braithwin grunted. ''Creewndithian beer is rough and sour, but if you stick with it it won't betray you the morning after. *Hael!*''

They drank, Horn barely taking a sip of his—he had tried this beer aboard Shembo's ship and concluded that it must be an acquired taste. Then Braithwin sank into a chair facing him and crossed his legs.

''The whole story!'' he commanded. ''And don't make it too fancy, hear?''

''Why Earth?'' Braithwin muttered when Horn had finished. ''Why *Earth*, of all the planets in the galaxy? If someone was hunting him, he could have been safe here, where he could have had a hundred armed men to watch him day and night—just by asking for them! But of course he was not the man to set overmuch store by simple safety. . . .''

''You knew him personally?'' ventured Horn. ''I wish I had done.''

''He was a cousin of mine—he and his brother Jan. I have sent for his brother; it will be well that he is told of his brother's death by me, before news gets to him by road of gossip. A freshener for your beer?''

Horn hastily covered his mug with his palm and shook his head. The girl poured for Braithwin and he drank as though trying to put out a fire in his belly.

"There must have been a reason for him going to Earth," he muttered as he set the mug aside, empty again. "There must have been a reason! You, Horn—do you know what it might have been?"

"Hardly," Horn said with a grimace. "So far, nobody's even told me what Talibrand was up to! A spaceman on Newholme—Dize, the one I mentioned as having helped me—he said if his identity had been known it would have handicapped his work, but as for what that work was . . ." He shrugged. "I was hoping you would tell me."

"Without asking leave of the Hereditary Council, I can't," Braithwin sighed. "I can only tell you what it was that made us propose him for citizenship of the galaxy. Your Newholmer friend was quite right—he was at first reluctant to accept the honor we pressed on him, because he said to be famous would hamstring his future plans. Then at last he agreed it would be a convenience to have the status of a citizen of the galaxy, with all the attendant power to draw upon in case of need, but insisted we withhold his name and appearance from the people and say merely that there was now a third citizen, beside Gayk and Yugus, so that if he was forced to reveal himself he would not be treated as an impostor."

Horn risked a further swig of his beer, found it much less unpleasant than at first, and took a healthy draft. "You were going to tell me what he did to secure the nomination," he prompted.

"Ah yes!" Braithwin held out his mug to the girl again, and she emptied the jug into it before departing in search of a fresh supply. "Well, he brought me proof that the eldest son of one of our noble families had been stolen away by a vicious and unmanly relative. He set out to trace the boy, and found him, and in the doing discovered that others had been taken, too: commoners' children, kidnapped by unscrupulous traders out of space. And they'd been taken out beyond Arthworld somewhere, transhipped, dyed blue—''

"Conditioned, and used to swell the supply of androids for Earth?" Horn leaned forward breathlessly.

"Precisely!" Braithwin rumbled. "But Lars did not rest satisfied with that one success. He determined to follow the whole terrible matter to its end. He uncovered other such happenings on half a dozen worlds, and in some cases was even able to restore the children to their families. So much did his discoveries revolt our council that we came close to barring the android traders altogether from Creew 'n Dith—for how could we ever know which of their androids might be a human child? But Jan Talibrand argued against this, saying it was the reverse of a tribute to his brother's work and would imply that he had not fully succeeded in his task, so we let things go on as before. We depend much on the tax we levy on the trade, of course, though I for one like it little and will have no androids in my employ. Still, you're from Earth, and doubtless you feel differently."

Horn shook his head. "In my family's household there is only one android, and he's been a sort of third parent to me since my birth. And, as I told you, I was started on my journey by androids. Well! What you've told me makes many things clear that baffled me, but I still find it hard to believe that even a few children could have—ah—vanished without causing a tremendous outcry."

Braithwin gave a mirthless chuckle. "To you from the tame planet Earth, doubtless it does seem strange. But here . . ." He reached to the floor beside his chair and lifted up a skull, ivory-yellow, its cruelly fanged jaws open in a dead snarl. From crown to snout it was fully the length of his forearm.

"I shot that beast on my own estate two years past, not a mile from where we're sitting. It had taken the slaughter of one of my retainers, a girl aged twelve. Ours is a wild world, Horn, even after centuries of occupation."

"So those missing children could have been assumed

victims of a killer beast. I follow you." Horn frowned. "And am I right to think that androids in general must have heard of what Lars had done?"

"Most certainly. Lars himself informed us that many had risked their lives to help him in the dim hope that they too might be found to have been stolen from human parents and not concocted in some chemical stew."

"Where *are* the androids made that are shipped through here?"

"On Arthworld, I suppose, or maybe further out. I told you, the less I have to do with android traders the better I'm pleased, and to me it's all one on what world they've set up their infernal cookery."

Horn said, fumbling, "I don't understand why androids should be shipped from so far away! I can understand it being very expensive to manufacture them on Earth, but I'd have thought the cost of transporting them all the way from Arthworld, or wherever, would have canceled the advantage out. There must be plenty of the requisite technicians on Vernier, for example. Or they could be recruited right here on Creew 'n Dith!"

"Unlikely," Braithwin grunted. "Some term it super-stition, but to me and many other folk of this world there's something you might call *unnatural* about men breathing, eating, sleeping, prone to our diseases, capable of speech, yet spawned of some artificial process. They're so nearly human, and yet they've been robbed of so much by their conditioning that they've been made empty. If I want something calm and rational, I'll settle for a machine. A man should enjoy a bit of healthy lust. He should be capable of love and hate! Though I suppose you think that's a barbaric attitude."

Horn chose his words with care. "Perhaps on your world you have a purpose to which such impulses can be put. On Earth they've turned inwards and gone sour. When I compare Dordy, the android, with a man like Coolin I can't help feeling that what the former lacks is mainly the capacity for self-indulgence which in the latter came out as vicious cruelty."

"Maybe," Braithwin shrugged. "Still, to us it was the most heartbreaking thing of all about those children Lars Talibrand rescued—to find that the devils who kidnapped them had made them as sterile and passionless as any android. Think of the hurt that caused to one man I know crippled in an accident—paralyzed—whose only son was returned to him and proved to lack the ability to carry on the line! I found him a brave youth to adopt, an orphan from among my own retinue, but it's not the same. Yes?"—this last to the girl who had served their beer, who during the conversation had reentered the room.

She said something in Creewndithian which Horn failed to catch, and Braithwin rose briskly.

"Jan Talibrand is here. He came at once to meet you when he heard the news."

Horn likewise stood up, just in time to confront the new arrival—a man so unlike he who had lain on Earth with a knife in his chest it was hard to credit that the two were brothers.

CHAPTER XIV

THIS WAS A LONG MAN—long of face, with dark eyes set close together beneath thin black brows; long of limb and body, long of hand and foot. Carefully dressed dark hair curled on his head. He wore clothes of the same style as did Braithwin, but elaborately embroidered with gold thread, and his belt was studded with jewels. He had a ring on his left thumb and jeweled buckles on his low shoes.

Removing a pair of large soft gloves, he offered Horn a hand that was very simply damp with sweat. His voice was low, and his command of Anglic as good as Braithwin's, though less colloquial.

"So you, sir, are the Earthman who cared enough about the fate of my unfortunate brother to bring news of him all the way from your home. My thanks, my sincere thanks—although the shock, of course, is terrible."

Horn stared him squarely in the face. After a moment he dropped his eyes and added, as though aware that he neither looked nor sounded like a man who had just been cut to the quick, "Though I must grant I had been steeling myself to hear he had risked his life once too often ever since he set about his foolhardy quest."

"Sit down and have some beer," Braithwin grunted. Talibrand complied, accepted a mug and held it while it was filled. He raised it in a ritual gesture.

"Lars Talibrand! Though he has departed may his honor remain!"

Horn seized his own mug, found it half-full, and drained it in the same toast, receiving a cordial nod from Braithwin. But there was something perfunctory about the sip which Talibrand took, and he immediately set his mug aside.

"Tell me how it happened, Mr. Horn!"

Horn complied, giving a much balder recital of the facts than he had given Braithwin, and at the end Talibrand shook his head and sighed.

"I warned him, over and over! Had he only listened to me he might have been alive and happy on our own estate—".

"Alive perhaps," Braithwin cut in with an edge of sarcasm. Horn had the distinct impression that he didn't like Jan Talibrand much. "But happy, no. He was only happy when searching out this evil he had stumbled on."

Talibrand didn't answer. Horn, studying his long pale face in an attempt to discern his real feelings, reflected that it must be embarrassing to be the brother of a citizen of the galaxy.

"Mr. Talibrand—" he began, and got no further.

"I beg your pardon," Talibrand said frostily. "My correct styling is not 'mister'—it is councillor. Hereditary

103

Councillor.''

Horn flushed and muttered something inaudible. A further point occurred to him. If primogeniture was the rule here, then presumably Lars Talibrand had been Jan's younger brother, an additional cause for resentment. Before he could say anything else, Talibrand was speaking again.

"Well, tomorrow I must hold the proper obsequies for my late brother. You are obviously unfamiliar with our customs, *Mr.* Horn"—he stressed the title heavily and scowled—"so I should explain that it is usual to hold a feast to honor the memory of the departed, at which only the family and those friends whom the deceased personally selected are ordinarily present. My brother of course left no directions more recent than his last departure from Creew 'n Dith, but I am sure he would have wished you to be added to the company had he been able to know of your existence." His dark eyes smoldered distantly.

Horn glanced at Braithwin, who gave him no clue. Well, it would be churlish to refuse, he supposed. He got to his feet and gave a half-bow.

"It will be an honor," he declared, and caught a tiny nod of approval from Braithwin at the corner of his eye.

"My home is at your disposal tonight and as long as you care to remain," Jan Talibrand had said, and taken his guest's consent for granted. He had ordered two of his retainers to bring Horn's belongings from the inn where he had been staying and loaded them into his lavishly appointed groundcar. It was a model that had been popular on Earth not more than two years before; Horn had seen nothing else to compare with it on Creew 'n Dith, and the cost of shipping it by interstellar freight must have been astronomical.

He had seized the moment when Talibrand was instructing his servants about the baggage to take his leave of Braithwin and put a question relevant to that groundcar. "I take it *Councillor* Talibrand is not poor?''

he had suggested, and a twinkle in Braithwin's eye had greeted the stress on the honorific.

"He has not perhaps the largest estate on Creew 'n Dith," was the reply. "But his great-grandfather had the foresight to inaugurate a well-appointed spaceport on his grounds and to leave much room for expansion. Consequently, though not richest in the land, this family is the wealthiest in terms of currency."

That accounted for a great deal.

The groundcar ran smoothly humming through the streets of the town—though it was one of the most populous on the planet, Horn could hardly bring himself to term it a city. They skirted the spaceport, where a consignment of androids was being discharged from a newly arrived vessel bearing an Arthworld registration. Watching them march across the port in groups of twenty on their way to confinement in a pen similar to the ones he had seen on Newholme, Horn wondered how many of them might be human beings disguised.

The idea revolted him. No wonder Lars Talibrand had been nominated to his high distinction for uncovering the ghastly secret!

"I gather, Councillor, that the port is part of your family estate?" he ventured. Talibrand, beside him on the soft long back seat of the car, nodded.

"This is the furthest corner of it from my residence. It does not disturb our peace and comfort."

Even if the Talibrand estate was not the largest here, it was impressive enough; the Horn family's estate, back on Earth, was a pocket handkerchief by comparison. They ran for miles over rough roads that tried the suspension of their vehicle, through woods, between fields in which tenant farmers labored behind draft animals for their own benefit—Horn had already found out about this system— while in others expensive robot farming machinery prepared the grounds for Talibrand's own crops.

Dusk was falling as they approached the house, or, as

the local usage preferred, the hall: a long rambling structure of stone roofed with timber, like Braithwin's in the town they had left behind. There were gardens before it, lawns of a soft green native moss, arbors, statues and fountains.

"We dine an hour past dark," Talibrand told him as they parted at the entrance of the house. "My retainers will escort you to your lodging. Anything you find in your room is at your disposal."

Horn found a great deal in his room, which was far more lavishly appointed than he would have expected from the outside appearance of the house or the long chilly echoing passages down which he had been led to it. Among other things there was a range of Creewndithian clothing in various sizes, and he gladly changed into the suit which fitted him best, recalling Dize's remark about an Earthman in the outworlds attracting as much attention as a parade band. He had just finished dressing when there was a timid tap at the door.

Assuming that one of the servants must be coming to call him to dinner, he drew back the bolt. A woman—no, a mere girl—slipped through the opening, shut the door promptly and leaned back against it, breathing hard as though recovering from tremendous effort. She was slim but shapely, as the belting of her white gown revealed; her long brown hair was caught up on her head by a gold clasp.

Horn was too surprised to speak, but in a moment she had mastered herself.

"Please forgive my intrusion!" she said in Anglic, her words fluent but strongly accented. "I will not detain you long—I dare not, for if Jan learns that I have shown myself to a stranger before putting on mourning garb . . .! I am Moda Talibrand. Quickly, please, the truth: is Lars indeed dead?"

Horn swallowed hard. "I—I'm afraid so. I found him on Earth with a knife in his heart."

She closed her eyes and swayed. Prepared to catch her

106

should she faint, Horn went on randomly, 'Ah ... Moda Talibrand? Are you his sister, then?''

"No!" Her eyes snapped open. "I'm—" her voice broke. "I'm his widow!''

She spun on her heel and ran from the room, Horn stretching out a vain hand to stop her.

He did not see her again until the following day; she was absent from dinner the same evening. But at the feast which was held at noon of the morrow she presided from one end of the immensely long table in the Great Hall, wearing a black gown with her hair in a tight black snood, toying with her food and every now and then raising her eyes to stare at the chair which stood empty at the other end with a black wreath on it framing a broken sword.

Horn barely had more appetite than she; stuffing one's belly and swilling gallons of the sour Creewndithian beer hardly struck him as an appropriate way to honor the memory of a dead hero. Granted, Jan Talibrand had opened the proceedings with a speech extolling his late brother's virtues, but it had the ring of something learned by rote and repeated parrot-fashion rather than a tribute from the heart. Later, Braithwin had also spoken, but at too great length for his audience, who grew restless and fidgeted. They consisted mainly of brawny men of young to middle age, a few elderly folk, and a great many matronly women in widow's weeds who sobbed loudly at intervals and then sought consolation in the beer-jugs.

Without warning, the youth whom Braithwin had pointed out to Horn as the adopted son of the paralyzed man they had spoken of the day before—presumably personally chosen by Lars Talibrand to attend his funeral feast—whose face had been growing darker and darker as the meal progressed, leapt to his feet and swept a space of ten feet clear of dishes, mugs and cutlery with a scabbarded sword before clambering on the table and tramping towards the empty chair at its head.

"Lars Talibrand!" he roared. "If no one else will speak

better of you then these drunken sots, then I must in the place of my crippled father whom you helped! Here they sit guzzling your beer and chomping joints of your meat and they're forgetting what they came here for!''

Horn, whose ear was barely as yet attuned to the Creewndithian speech, turned to Braithwin in the next chair, who told him in low tones what the youth was saying. Meantime, Jan Talibrand thrust back his chair, his brow like thunder.

"*Whose* beer?" he snapped. "*Whose* meat? *Whose* house and hospitality are you abusing?"

Horn needed no translation of that—the meaning was all too obvious.

"I'd get out of here if I were you," Braithwin said very softly. "There's going to be a fight, and—and I feel ashamed for my kinfolk!"

Indeed, Talibrand was shouting at his retainers, and one of them was running to fetch a sword. Some of the company, their food forgotten, were cheering and laughing drunkenly, while Moda Talibrand was leaning forward and her parted lips were moving, as though expressing a silent wish that all this could be a dream.

Braithwin thrust back his chair and rose, framing a scornful condemnation of such behaviour, but it was too late. With a cry of fury, the youth had leapt from the table and confronted Talibrand, and up and down the table there was an unholy racket, as women rose and headed for the door and men argued unsoberly about the rights and wrongs of the contestants. When he saw that other sword had been drawn, Horn decided that Braithwin's advice was correct and slipped away, shaking from head to foot. The noise of the growing brawl followed him down the corridors to his room.

"Lars Talibrand!" he whispered to the air. "Whoever's fit to follow in your footsteps, it doesn't seem to be one of your own family!"

He thrust open his door and checked in mid-stride, thinking he must have made a mistake, for the room was not empty. A bent figure in a drab gown was sitting on the edge of one of the chairs. He apologized and made to withdraw.

"I beg forgiveness, Mr. Horn!" the stranger wheezed— an old woman. Very, *very* old! Horn halted, marveling; he had never seen anyone on Earth so bent and fragile. "But I had to speak to you about my son Lars—Lars who I'm told is dead!"

She struggled to stand up and finally succeeded. For the first time the light fell on her face, and with shattering amazement Horn saw that the face of Lars Talibrand's mother—was blue.

CHAPTER XV

"PLEASE!" said the old woman in supplication. "Please! I am very old, but I am not mad!"

Horn approached slowly and sat down on the edge of the bed facing her as she lowered her aged bones once more into the chair, closing her eyes as she did so. "I didn't say anything, granny," he murmured. "Please explain."

Rapidly, confusedly, with many repetitions but obvious overwhelming sincerity, she told him the story of the Talibrands.

Barg Talibrand, father of Jan and Lars, had been a *simpler* man than either of his sons; that was her actual term, but Horn glossed it as meaning less intelligent. When his wife became too ill to endure his violent love-making after bearing him the elder son, Jan, he had gone down to the spaceport one day and picked out a female android to satisfy him instead—one who, as well as being buxom and comely, was relatively well educated, could cook, make clothes, sing and speak passable Anglic: all in all, not unfit to be a concubine in one of the noblest families on Creew 'n Dith.

Horn had never heard of a female android before. As the tale progressed, a possible reason why they were no longer shipped onward via here to Earth emerged.

When this female android—allegedly as sterile as the males, an obvious advantage in a society where rights of succession were jealously guarded—conceived a child, Barg Talibrand had at first boasted of his unprecedented virility; he joked about fathering a baby on a woman who couldn't have one. Then the strangeness of the event began to prey on his mind, and some member of a cadet branch of the family, seeing a chance to get the thick-witted Barg under his thumb, fed him a superstitious explanation and preached impending doom.

Raging, Barg banned the transit of female androids through his spaceport. Bit by bit, he came to accept that instead of being blessed with incredible powers of generation he was cursed, and at last he died in a haze of insanity.

The whole affair was hushed up, and as soon as he was old enough to run the estate, Jan cleared out the parasites who had sponged on his father during the years of decline. He would have liked to remove the last vestige of the tragedy by doing away with the android woman. By then, though, Lars had developed into the kind of forceful personality Horn had imagined, capable of outfacing anyone else in the family, and defiantly accepting his improbable ancestry had sworn to have the life of anyone who harmed his mother.

Of course, directly he learned the truth about the kidnapped children who were being disguised as androids, he realized his mother too must have been human and stolen away in a similar fashion. And there lay the motive which had driven him from world to world, hounding the android traders who had grown fat on the profit from such crimes.

No wonder Jan was jealous! To be surpassed by a brother who was not only younger, but a bastard to boot . . .!

The door of the room slammed open, and Horn leapt up in alarm. Jan Talibrand stood before him, panting, with blood trickling out of his left sleeve. There was more blood on the naked sword he held. He barked in Creewndithian at the ancient crone, who covered her face and rocked back and forth in rhythm with an outburst of sobs.

He shouted at her again, and she made a tearful answer. Talibrand spat on the floor and rounded on Horn.

"So, you lickspittle Earthling! You abuse my hospitality by eavesdropping, skulking in corners, bribing my retinue to unearth scandalous lies—is that how it is?"

The old woman cried that she had not been bribed, that she had come voluntarily to Horn, and his face distorted with animal rage.

"In that case I'm finished with you!" he snarled. "You've been a mark of my father's shame for far too long. And now Lars can't protect you any more—!"

He choked and strode forward. His sword crashed down with lunatic violence, and it split the old woman's skull from crown to nape.

Appalled by the futile savagery of the deed, Horn was for a moment too overcome to react. At last he forced out, "Your father's shame is nothing to the shame of that, Jan Talibrand!"

"Shame? How dare you?" Talibrand roared. "There's no shame in disposing of an old and worn-out android—only common sense."

"But she wasn't an android!" Fury drove Horn plunging on. "She can't have been—not if she bore a child!"

"I say she was," Talibrand gritted, and raised his sword to the level of Horn's heart. "And it is not seemly for a guest to insult his host by calling him a liar."

"I don't believe I care to enjoy the hospitality of one who kills old defenseless women and threatens unarmed

111

men, made brave only by possession of a sword!" Horn made each successive word crack like a whip, and Talibrand's face went perfectly white.

"Come then!" he said softly. "They tell me you're clever with a blade—that lately you killed your challenger in a duel. But Coolin was a decadent Earthling like yourself. Let's find out how you compare with a man of Creew 'n Dith!"

In that instant Horn was finally certain of something he had barely dared to suspect before. Since his arrival on Creew 'n Dith, he had told no one but Braithwin the full story of his departure from home. Certainly, in the bald account he had given Jan Talibrand of the circumstances surrounding Lars's death, he had never spoken Coolin's name.

So while Lars Talibrand hunted evil men from world to world, his brother was hand-in-glove with his mortal enemies.

But there was no time for thought now. At sword-point he was being chivvied along the passages that led to the great hall. There had indeed been fighting here, more than he would have imagined: there a door showed splinters of bright white wood, here someone had had to spill sand on a patch of blood. From outside came the occasional snap of a projectile weapon, and there were no servants in sight. Horn guessed that the last of the guests were having to be driven forcibly off the premises.

"There's a sword!" Talibrand halted opposite the door to the vestibule which connected the great hall and the outside air. The hall itself was a chaos of overset chairs and smashed crockery, which no one had yet started to clear away. Not a little nervous, for the walk from his room had given him chance to overcome his first uncontrollable rage at Talibrand's murder of the old woman, Horn hesitated. It would be better to stand his ground in the vestibule, he decided; it was adequately large, perhaps twenty feet square, and he could avoid the risk of losing his footing on the debris with which the hall

112

was littered.

As unhurriedly as he could, he advanced to pick up the weapon Talibrand had indicated, and went still a pace or two further before turning. He needed a moment to get the feel of the sword. Dismayed, he discovered it was heavy and cumbersome compared with the ones he was accustomed to on Earth, but here there were no such niceties as the chance to balance a strange blade with a convenient grindstone.

"Your last chance, stranger from Earth," Talibrand said, planting his feet apart and scowling. "Confess you're a booby devoid of decent manners and I'll let you depart with your life."

"I don't believe you," Horn grunted. "You'd be afraid to have anyone tell the truth about you—granny-killer!"

One heartbeat later he was half an inch from death.

Here was no mannerly fencer like Coolin, rendered vulnerable by his eagerness for blood. Despite his foppish appearance, Talibrand was a genuine fighter, and though he must have been tired by his previous encounters, to which the slash on his left arm testified, his movements were fast, economical and controlled. Also Horn judged, he did not lack stamina. *This* was not a match that would end quickly on a sophisticated trick.

For a while he contented himself wholly with defense, his sword always arriving—though he himself once or twice expected it not to—in time to turn Talibrand's edge. They closed, parted, closed again, locked hilts in a brief trial of strength during which he thought he could read in his opponent's eyes grudging respect for his competence, and broke by unspoken agreement into a series of conventional thrusts and parries. But during it he knew Talibrand was maneuvering him, and dared not look behind to see why, only realizing the truth when his foot slipped in a wet patch on the floor—blood, perhaps, shed by one of the reluctantly departing guests—and he came within an ace of overbalancing.

With a gasp, he jumped back, touching the wall with

one elbow, and used the instant Talibrand needed for recovery to dart aside. Was Talibrand tiring, was his recovery slow? Horn could not tell; he was too busy fending off the next attack.

Talibrand tried to lock hilts again, and he avoided the clash. He was pounds the lighter, and even though he had hardened up considerably since he looked with distaste at his own soft body in the hotel suite on Earth, he was probably not as strong.

And that was what was going to tell in the end.

Over Talibrand's shoulder he saw that they were no longer alone. Both doors to the vestibule were crowded with watchers: retainers with long guns on their shoulders, back from clearing the grounds of the visitors, servants interrupted on the way to clear the great hall of the mess on its floor . . . and Moda Talibrand.

She was gazing open-lipped and tense, hands clasped as though in prayer. That was all Horn saw in the instant he was distracted, and it was almost too much—Talibrand was on him, blade raised high for a killing blow!

Moda cried out; he dodged desperately, and as he did so his sword—almost undirected by his will—touched Talibrand's already wounded left arm and he felt it grate as it rubbed on living bone.

Talibrand's mouth opened in what began to be a scream, and changed without the drawing of another breath into a shouted order as he saw that Horn's sword could reach his exposed belly before his own could rise to meet it. Something struck Horn across the back of the neck, and he went sprawling, his sword lost. Two of Talibrand's retainers dragged him to his feet again and held his arms in an iron grasp.

What now? Does he have me spitted like a pig? But was it rational to expect a man like Jan Talibrand to fight to the finish?

Dazed, he looked about him and discovered that one person at least among the company shared his view of

Talibrand. For Moda was advancing on her brother-in-law, her gown swishing at every step. She halted before him and deliberately spat upwards into his face.

"Coward!" she said—in Anglic. A glance at Horn left no room for doubt as to why she had selected the language.

His eyes burning, Talibrand wiped the spittle from his cheek.

"Coward!" she repeated. "Losing in a fair fight, and you get your dirty hirelings to save your worthless life!" She stamped her small foot, blazing with rage. "Oh, If I were only a man!"

"You're not even a natural woman," said Talibrand coldly. "To wed and bed with the child of an android—*faugh!* You disgust me, and I'm not surprised that you take the side of a stranger against your own family! So how do you enjoy being told that he has killed your husband's mother? I found her in his room with her skull split!"

The incredible lie galvanized Horn. "Why, you—!" he began, but one of the men who held him clapped a broad palm over his mouth, and though he tried by biting into the flesh to drive the hand away, he failed.

Offering his new wound to be looked at by attendants, Talibrand was continuing. "I shan't simply have him killed, if that's what you're thinking. A clean quick death would be better than he deserves. For him there is only one logical, beautiful fate. . . ."

He chuckled suddenly, and the sound chilled Horn's blood.

"Oh yes! You're going to *hate* your life before it snuffs out!"

CHAPTER XVI

When Horn had exhausted himself in struggling, he was
dragged through the house to a dark, stinking room; here
an old man as shriveled as the mummy of a bat trembled
up to him and broke a capsule of something pungent
under his nose, and his consciousness shattered into
fragments.

He woke once to jolting darkness and the sound of men
yelling orders, but could not make sense of what he heard;
then a second time to find himself floating under nil
gravity, bouncing very slowly from side to side of a cuboid
cage of thongs. They were smeared with something sticky
and unpleasant, and a fetid animal stench assailed him;
he was glad to flee into oblivion again.

But that was the last time he managed to do so. His
third waking was on a patch of gravely soil under a blank
white sky, and he was shocked conscious by the impact of
a bucket of icy water.

"On your feet, you!" grunted the man who had thrown
it—a total stranger with a bald head and a straggly fair
beard. Too dazed to think of not obeying, Horn tried to
rise, and found he was too weak to lift his own weight. He
gave a groan.

"Idiots, starving him like that," the stranger muttered.
He reached out and hoisted Horn upright so easily he was
astonished. He caught a glimpse of his own arm, on which
stringy muscles knotted with effort stood out under pallid
skin, and then the stranger was hustling him down a slope
and he could barely keep his balance.

Summoning enough energy for delay, if not for re-
sistance, Horn tried to take in his surroundings. The sky
was pale with high driven clouds; the ground too was
whitish, and here and there it sparkled. Salt-pans? That

fitted. A trickle of the water that had been poured over him ran into his mouth, and that was salty. Distantly he heard the soughing of ocean against a beach.

Over to his right, four battered and rusty ships pointed their blunt noses at the sky. Men and women dressed in coarse badly cut garments of a fabric like tweed, guns and daggers belted at their waists, were going to and fro among them.

"Where—where have you brought me?" Horn croaked.

"Don't waste energy trying to talk!" his escort rapped. "Just keep moving along!"

Horn stumbled on. Salty gravel got into his shoes and cut his feet. Soon, he was compelled to scramble up a dune, though grass-like plants slashed his shins. And over the crest of the dune . . .

Camps. Compounds. Stretching for miles. Glittering huts built from blocks of crude rock-salt, patched here and there with brown. Among them huge vats steaming towards the sky, a smear of blueness staining the ground nearby. As Horn managed to focus his eyes, the blur separated into a horde of naked children.

By each of the vats a brawny human was ladling out portions of steaming mush into bowls. More docile than animals, the children waited in dutiful lines to receive their share. Horn had a chance to see them closely as his companion hurried him along a well-beaten path bordering the compounds but separated from them by a pit and a high barbed fence. He raged impotently within himself at the sluggishness of both mind and body; he knew, tinglingly, that what he was seeing was crucially important, but he could only register it with passive eyes that now and then blurred as a last drop of the water he had been drenched with drained out of his hair. His body ached everywhere, his throat was sore, he was bruised and feeble and all his joints were swollen. He must have been tossed around during his trip here like a sack of rubbish.

At the intersection of this path with another a sharp

female voice hailed them, and a woman with an air of authority strode up to them. Desperate, Horn tried to memorize her face, but a fit of dizziness overcame him and all he could cope with was the words she uttered. At least she was speaking Anglic, not some outworld tongue he was ignorant of.

"That's the one Talibrand sent out from Creew 'n Dith, I suppose! Miserable-looking specimen, isn't he? Didn't they even pipe any food into him on his way here"

"Doesn't look like it," Horn's escort grunted. "He's so weak he can barely stand up. I guess Talibrand must have it in for him in a big way!"

"That's for sure." The woman consulted a sheaf of dirty paper she was carrying. "Which way did he come in, anyhow—on Rynalman's route?"

"That's right. The Arthworld way. Why?"

"We have to send him back by a different one. Talibrand insisted. Hmmm—let's see now. Oh yes, that's pretty convenient. He can go through Vernier, with the batch Firgal's processing right now from out Lostworld way. Take him down and get him blued up, and stick him in with the others. Plurivel's going to Vernier this trip and he can cram in a few more, I guess."

"How's about the rest of it?" the man demanded. "Conditioning, and sterilization?"

"Conditioning not," the woman answered, riffling through her papers. "The way I hear it, Talibrand wants this to hurt as much as possible—says someone'll take a whip to him right away if he starts claiming to be a human being, or maybe have his brain pithed. I don't seem to have anything here about sterilization, though...."

That's me they're discussing. The fact seeped slowly into Horn's awareness. *That's the "logical, beautiful" fate Talibrand planned for me!* He glanced around wildly, seeking a way of escape, but when his escort took hold of his arm he lacked even the strength to throw off the grip.

The woman shuffled her papers together with a shrug. "Well, what the hell's the difference whether he's

118

sterilized or not? All he'll be getting from now on is android company, and the kind of human woman who orders
an android with the urge intact isn't the kind likely to
risk having children by anybody. Okay, move him along.''

Moaning, trying to struggle but betrayed in every
feeble attempt by his own wasted muscles, Horn was
forced along until they reached a large low prefabricated
building where—as the woman had put it—Firgal was
''processing.'' The sight drained Horn of all power to act;
he could only absorb the terrible truth that Lars
Talibrand must have learned, the truth which meant he
had to follow the android trade to its terminal on Earth
even though he risked his life.

Firgal was processing children. Human children.
Scores—perhaps a hundred—were crowded into a wire
cage at one end of the building: peaked, mostly naked and
revealing skins of every human shade from stark white to
deepest brown, aged between six months and six years.
Horn's head rang with their screaming. Women in dirty
gowns dragged each in turn from the cage and tossed them
on a table, where a man in a full-head mask stabbed them
with a hypodermic, rolled them over to sever the nerves
governing the sexual reflexes with a fast blast from a self-
sterilizing light-scalpel, and waved them onwards to
make room for the next.

Horn's grasp of reality failed under the shocking
impact of the spectacle. His eyes rolled upwards in their
sockets and he slumped into a faint. When he woke up, his
skin was a brilliant blue.

Detachedly, he was aware that this time he had been
better looked after; he had been fed intravenously and his
bruises and aches had been attended to. But that was only
something he turned his mind to in order to distract
himself from the appalling sight of his own hand.

Blue? I can't believe it! But—but it is my hand!

They had taken his clothes and draped him in one of the
standard android ponchos. He swept it off and saw that

119

the blue stretched unbroken from head to foot.

In memory he heard again the harsh voice of the woman who had said, "Someone'll take a whip to him right away if he starts claiming to be a human being, or maybe have his brain pithed." Despair that would not lift clamped over his mind as he realized how true that was—how often back on Earth friends of his had complained of having to return a newly bought android under guarantee and train a replacement from scratch.

And who had the right to order his brain pithed, the higher nerve-centers destroyed so that he was fit only for repetitive menial chores—the woman in charge here, Plurivel the captain of the ship he was being sent out on? Yes, of course! Anyone could, any human being! Androids were legally property! And—he had to shut his eyes as he swayed, then instantly to re-open them as the imagined vision of Jan Talibrand's glee besieged him—wasn't that the climax Lars's traitor-brother must be hoping for?

Anyhow, with whom could he share his new and terrible knowledge? He was surrounded by a crowd of young male androids, presumably the load destined for Vernier and eventually Earth, but they still displayed the aftereffects of recent intensive conditioning, glazed eyes, streels of drool hanging from the corners of their slack mouths, wet stains on the hems of their ponchos. In that state they were barely aware of the most violent pain, and wholly incapable of following a complicated sentence.

Sick, he drew his poncho around him again, for he was shivering, and sat down. So this was how his foolhardy venture was doomed to end! He had done as he hoped and made the same discovery as Lars Talibrand, and he was not even going to be accorded a quick clean death.

For everything pointed to a single conclusion. There were no android factories anywhere off Earth. There were no "imported androids." There were only human children stolen from their homes.

He remembered the fringe of uncertainty on the map

Dize had loaned him, where the cartographers had had to mark some of the names of inhabited planets against more than one star. That was the zone where so-called android traders gathered their human harvest, among worlds too poor and struggling to afford their own starships and interstellar communicators, around which the frontier of colonial expansion ebbed and flowed so that it was seldom certain whether their inhabitants had survived or not, far away on uncaring Earth.

He gained insight into the manner of that harvest from seeing a ship on the port when he and the rest of Plurivel's load were being herded into dank echoing holds for their trip to Vernier. The other ship had been attacked and defended; its plates were splattered with shot, and an explosion had distorted two of the drive-tubes. Horn pictured the traders dropping from the sky above some crude village, where people cut off from the mainstream of galactic commerce were trying to recreate some semblance of civilization, seizing their prey, being vainly challenged and making good their escape under cover of advanced weaponry bought with their evil profits.

Once caught, the children—selected because they were too young to understand what was happening—would be brought here or to some similar encampment for "processing." If it chanced that some captive was precocious, and might later recall details that would give away the raiders, then he (or she, but the demand for female androids had greatly diminished) was ruthlessly brainwashed into amnesia. Losses in transit were highest among this group, and most of them were sold off before they reached Earth, for the treatment left them dull-witted and surly.

All this Horn picked up in dribs and drabs, some by building on what the androids he was shipped with could tell him, some from hints dropped by trained androids with whom he came into contact during transhipment on Vernier. At first he was amazed that not one of them questioned what they had been told about their origin in a

121

factory; then he realized that the truth about human birth is incredible to many children, and anyhow neither manufacture nor birth was accessible to conscious memory. They might intellectually, much later, learn to wonder about what they had been told, but the story had been so effectively hammered home that at present they clung to it like a religious dogma.

They knew what caused their blueness, and talked freely about it—a semiliving suspension of protein which on reaching the epidermis reacted with one of the normal skin secretions. It would go on renewing itself until death.
. Sizing up his chance companions, he realized after a while that he had not yet run across any who might later make a Dordy. He could see many who might develop like Berl into a skilled manual worker, but where were the seeds of the intelligence, the inquiring attitude, the insight into character Dordy had displayed?

That too he figured out. He was among a batch of averagely intelligent androids with good mechanical skills and a generally calm temperament. Those who rated above this level received special treatment, advanced education on some planet whose name he could not establish, and double the normal conditioning to restrain their nervy, unreliable personalities.

That too was something Lars Talibrand must have discovered. Perhaps he had received the all-important clues from one of those exceptional androids? He had trusted Dordy on sight; something must have persuaded him that he could confide in a blue-skinned stranger. . . .

It was bitter consolation to Horn to realize that in fact even though Talibrand had followed the trail clear to Earth where the armor of his galactic citizenship was useless, he had never learned so much about the android trade as his successor. He had never, after all, seen it from the inside. But there seemed to be no use to put that knowledge to!

Growing desperate, he tried to arouse the interest of his companions, but for them human beings were simply

osses who tossed them around from planet to planet and
eat them when they refused to obey. Why should they
eel attracted to the idea that they were themselves
uman? Hopeless! Hopeless! Trapped in his blue
isguise, Horn more than once wondered how long he
ould resist the temptation of suicide.

On Vernier the original group was split up, Horn being
ut in with the higher grades, and together with several
trangers from another ship they were carried somewhere
lse. Horn couldn't identify the world; all he saw of it was
he edge of a spaceport, and the hard-faced dealers who
ame to look the new arrivals over declined to answer any
uestions, merely studied their prospective purchases. At
n auction he was bought by a ship's captain who treated
ndroids more harshly than either Larrow or Shembo, for
e transported them without artificial gravity in the
olds, to economize on power. That was the most
errifying experience yet for Horn: to float, as he must
ave done on the journey out from Creew 'n Dith when
iost of the time he was mercifully unconscious, in a
pringy cage of leather thongs while all round his
ompanions moaned and cried out and sometimes
omited foul liquids that drifted weightlessly until they
truck the thongs.

Afterwards he thought he must have gone insane for a
vhile, because his next clear perceptions were of a
paceport. Open sky above, shedding a little chilly rain;
wnings flapping as they were erected; everyone shiver-
ig and huddled together. How like it was to the time he
ad first seen a cargo of androids at the port on
ewholme—

Newholme?

Bewildered, he stared about him as though scales had
illen from his eyes. Hope bloomed in his dark mind like
ie outburst of a nova. This was the same port on
ewholme he had seen before, and human beings were
pproaching the android compound talking loudly about
ie selection of a supercargo for the voyage to Earth, and

among them was . . .

Horn struggled to his feet, thrusting aside those of his fellows who clung to him for warmth.

"Dize!" he shouted. "*Dize!*"

CHAPTER XVII

As HORN struggled desperately through the press of androids to reach the side of the pen, he saw Dize check in puzzlement, heard him say to one of his two companions, "Kyer, did I hear somebody calling me?"

Kyer! The name that had been signed to the letter he'd found among Cavelgrune's belongings! He'd never expected to encounter him, or any other of Talibrand's confederates, on this voyage—he'd assumed that when the letter, along with everything else he owned, fell into Talibrand's hands emergency warnings would have been sent out. Could it be that the traders had too efficiently accomplished their assigned task of "losing" him among anonymous androids, so that not even someone in Kyer's position knew which consignment he was traveling with?

The dealer was a little man with sharp eyes. His face revealed anxiety as he glanced into the android compound and rapidly away again.

"I didn't hear anything, Mr. Dize," he said. "Except the regular chatter. Well, shall we move on to the next batch?"

Frantically Horn clawed his way the last few paces to the fence, seized it in both hands and rattled it until the supports rang. "Dize! *Dize!* Come over here and take a look at me!"

Kyer spotted him now, and his expression changed to one of pure horror. The third man in the group, a uniformed member of the port authority staff, seemed

124

bewildered and was glancing blankly from one to another of his companions.

Dawning comprehension showed on Dize's face. He strode over to the wire and stared at Horn, frowning as though trying to imagine his features unstained by android blue. All of a sudden his jaw dropped.

"By all the galaxies, it's Derry Horn! I'd know you anywhere! What in space is this bastard Kyer up to, trying to sell you off as an android?"

"Stop him!" Horn shouted, and lunged forward against the wire as though he could tear an opening with his bare hands. Kyer had spun on his heel and fled, terror lending wings to his feet.

"After him!" Dize screamed at the port official. "Don't let him get away! That's a friend of mine in there—been kidnapped and painted blue!"

But the other man's reactions were too slow; the whole outburst had left him dazed. He set off in Dize's wake at a lumbering run, but long before they managed to catch him Kyer had made good his escape among a crowd of passengers assembling for a departing flight.

Dize returned, panting and cursing, and snapped at the official to open the cage quickly and let Horn out.

"Bastard!" he said thickly. "Won't get away with this, I promise you—if I have to stand guard at the port myself, I'll make sure he doesn't get off Newholme! Here, come and tell me what's happened, Horn ... Horn, are you ill?"

His voice changed and he took a step forward in alarm as Horn stumbled through the compound gate.

"I'm—I'm all right," he whispered. "It's just that I never expected to ..."

He felt his eyes stinging and a lump rose in his throat. There was no way of making it clear to anyone who hadn't suffered his recent terrible experiences how glad he was to be free.

The official broke in. "Mr. Dize, you can't just help yourself to one of these androids! They're bonded cargo in transit, and I have to answer for—''

"Android be damned, blasted and perditioned!" Dize bellowed, putting his arm around Horn's shoulder as he closed his eyes and swayed. "This is Derry Horn of Horn & Horn Robots, and I shipped out from Earth with him only a month ago!"

The official's eyes bulged. His mouth worked but no sound emerged.

"Let 'em all out!" Horn whispered. "They're all human, same as I am. I've been all the way to the planet where they start their trip. There isn't a factory there, only a place where they bring human children to be sterilized and dyed blue and conditioned into believing they're a manufactured product. That's what Lars Talibrand found out—that's why the traders had him killed!"

"*What?*"

"What he's been through must have turned his mind," said the port official solicitously. "I guess you'd better call a doctor and—"

Horn fixed him with burning eyes. "Crazy, am I? You'll see! How big a cut do you take on these *people* Kyer's been buying and selling?"

He rounded on Dize. "Look, I've got to get to someone in authority, fast! I must get back to Creew 'n Dith and fix the bastard who did this to me. I'm going to take him apart with my own two hands."

There was no anger in the words—only a cold fury which made Dize shiver visibly.

"Captain Larrow's waiting for me to load the cargo for the next trip," he said finally. "Hang on while I get a message through and tell him he's going to be one man short, and I'll do exactly what you want!"

"Well, I don't really see that there's much we can do, Mr. Horn," said the portly lawforce commissioner. "I do naturally sympathize, don't misunderstand me. It must be dreadful to be kidnapped and disguised as one of the artificial—"

"Stop saying that!" Horn blazed. "I tell you there aren't any 'artificial' androids going through your port! They're human!"

"Ah—*yes*," the commissioner said soothingly, in a tone which implied that the sooner Horn was taken to a psychiatrist the sooner he'd give up that nonsensical delusion. "But you see you can't file suit from here against the person you allege to be responsible, and no crime has been committed in Newholmer law. Even this person Kyer ... well, to be frank, Mr. Horn!" He stumbled over the formal mode of address, as though calling anyone with a blue skin "mister" grossly offended him. "You have no evidence that he was aware of your identity have you?"

"So why did he take to his heels when Horn exposed him?" Dize barked.

"Really, Mr. Dize, if *I* were to see an apparently deranged android being let out of the compound and hear him promise to go for me, I think I'd quite likely make myself scarce just as he did." The commissioner settled comfortably in his chair. "We'll carry out the necessary inquiries, I can assure you of that. But I can't commit myself any further."

"Let's get out of here," Horn said morosely, and rose.

Dize caught up with him on the way to the street, scowling. "Why, that fathead!" he muttered. "Wish I could have him aboard ship with me for a week or two!"

"I should have expected this," Horn sighed. "People have been used all their lives to accepting a blue skin as proof in itself of android origin. What's more, the commissioner probably knows perfectly well that if something did happen to upset the android trade, Newholme and Creew 'n Dith and all the rest of the worlds through which the cargoes are staged would be cutting their chief economic lifeline to Earth. Earth's so stinking rich there's just about nothing else except androids they care to import in quantity!"

"Yes, but ..." Dize swallowed hard. "I mean, if I hadn't met you in this condition, I guess I'd have found it hard to believe, too, but now you tell me I've been shipping real humans all these years, and—and I feel I want to throw up!"

"You can comfort yourself with the notion that most people on Earth are in a state by now where they'd cheerfully sell their own children for androids if it meant saving themselves a bit of trouble." They had reached the street now and were walking along together, attracting many curious glances from passers-by.

"All right, but—but so far I can't make it clear to myself how the sheer volume of the supply is kept up!" Dize grunted. "I mean, we carry nearly ten thousand a year ourselves, aboard Larrow's ship!"

"Now, it's all working pretty easily," Horn said. He'd had plenty of time, during the long lonely days shut up among the androids, to work out the way it had to be.

"Part of the supply, but only part, comes from worlds close to here, like Creew 'n Dith, where there are still enough wild animals to make it convincing that the kids might have been killed and eaten by them. I've no way of being sure, but I suspect that until Lars Talibrand came along the proportion was much higher—after all, the shorter the distances you have to transport them, the more profitable your victims must be.

"The main source, though, is way, way out. Think for a moment. Think of that chart of the inhabited galaxy you showed me, with the names marked by guesswork out beyond Arthworld. How long has it been since anyone on Newholme was sufficiently interested to send out a ship and check on the accuracy of those maps? A century?"

"Well—ah ..." Dize looked embarrassed. "Yes, I reckon you'd have some difficulty getting the funds appropriated for an exploring ship these days, just to go check on the accuracy of a map."

"Same on Earth, only worse. We fixed the troubles which made people want to emigrate, like overcrowding and poverty. The pressure came off Newholme and you settled down to enjoy life, as was only natural. Here, and on Creew 'n Dith and probably on Lygos and Vernier and all the rest of them, people with a whole new planet to develop stopped being interested in what was going on out there at the frontier.

"But the sort of restless types who are dissatisfied enough to pioneer a new planet are much more prepared to accept the nuisance and inconvenience and even danger of moving on to still another strange world. So long as they manage to keep their ships intact, of course— it takes a colossal technical foundation to manufacture new ones. In the past century or so a dozen or more new worlds may have been opened up, by people who apart from their ships are living in a kind of Stone Age! Nobody knew where they would end up, even on the planets they set out from, and if they wore their ships out and couldn't send news back, who'd realize the frontier had engulfed yet another star?"

"I get you," Dize nodded. "Yes, it hangs together okay."

"And that, of course, is where the traders collect their supply of so-called androids, by raiding isolated settlements which can't report what's going on because they're completely cut off from the old-established worlds."

"Do you mean there never *were* such things as real androids?"

Horn shook his head. "Of course not. I know for a certainty that androids really are made, back on Earth. But the skill and training involved must be fantastic, and the cost when they were first introduced must have been astronomical. But because Earth is so rich, and because human beings always like to outshine their neighbors by having something that'll make them jealous, I guess the demand must have been tremendous. So someone— maybe one day we'll find out who—presumably said to himself, 'I know the answer to this!' And he organized a supply of 'imported' androids."

"But if the skills required are so advanced, how could he have made people believe—?"

Horn cut Dize's interruption short. "Once a thing's been done, it's far easier to repeat it than it was to do it the first time. I was fooled for ages, because intrinsically there's nothing absurd about the idea that someone might have packed the equipment for an android factory aboard a starship and gone off to some world where he could train his own operators and just help himself to the necessary raw materials by going out and digging them up. The guy who started this android trade probably used exactly that argument as a cover.

"At first, I imagine, it would just have been a kidnapping racket. The price was high enough so that the profit on a few victims would have more than paid for the cost of going out and getting them. Then as androids started to be mass-produced it would have become necessary to draw on a source where a whole shipload could be had at one blow—these isolated frontier worlds I just mentioned."

"But someone must have asked awkward questions!" Dize insisted.

"Why? All of a sudden, look! Here's a profitable commercial item in great demand on Earth. Overnight, worlds which formerly were too poor to buy anything from Earth except the most basic essentials became able to purchase luxuries as well. So the kidnapping racket turns into a full-scale slave trade, and but for the fact that someone was foolish enough to revert to the old-fashioned notion of stealing away kids from a relatively advanced planet, right under Lars Talibrand's nose on Creew 'n Dith, it might have gone on indefinitely.

"You see, the masterminds of the trade are far from stupid. You know Shembo personally, don't you? Have you talked with him since I last saw you?"

Dize shook his head. "Our schedules haven't crossed on Newholme lately."

"Well, two of Kyer's associates were sent to try and

130

kidnap me from his ship, and when Shembo prevented them they killed themselves."

"I heard about that!" Dize said, startled. "Two dead bodies found lying on the port, right? They'd taken poison and their ID had been stolen. You say they were connected with Kyer? Why didn't you tell the commissioner, then?"

"Since my meeting with Coolin, I'm not inclined to trust lawforce officers," Horn grunted. "That's not the point. What I'm driving at is that it takes fierce conditioning to insure that your subordinates kill themselves rather than be unmasked. I've no doubt that anyone who agrees to take part in the android trade is threatened with that, and also with the possibility that if he betrays the organization he'll be thrown in with a batch of androids, as I was, but with his brain pithed so he can't give away any secrets.

"Besides that precaution, the masterminds compartmentalize the trade so efficiently that I'm willing to bet you've never known for sure where any of the androids you shipped had originated. Right?"

"Well, on the manifests ..." Dize checked himself. "No, you're quite right. Never thought of that before. I've never dealt with anyone who'd actually been on the world which the androids were attributed to, only with middlemen like myself and Shembo."

"Right. The end of the trade closest to the point of origin is carefully confined to people conditioned against talking. The androids themselves are not only kidnapped when they're too young to talk, if possible, but also have their brains thoroughly washed. Then they're separated in transit—not one of the group I started off with from wherever I was blued up is there on the port at the moment. The rest have been scattered to different ships approaching Earth via different outworlds."

"But it must cost a fortune for every single one, to raise them and train them!" Dize exploded. "Androids arrive here as youths, not children—I don't know how old you

131

are, but you're obviously over twenty, and even so I wouldn't have remarked on you specially for your age because I've quite often seen high-quality androids go through who were out of their teens. Though most, of course, are around twelve to fifteen, near as I can judge. Either way, it must cost a hell of a lot to—keep 'em in store so long!"

"Pennies," Horn grunted. "I've been in among them, I've talked to them, and I *know*. This was one of the things they started to build towards directly it became obvious they were involved in a long-term operation. The more completely an android is trained—to handle a complicated job like Dordy's, for example—the better the price is proportionately. You can feed and train one of these kids on the lonely outworlds where nothing costs anything except going out and getting it for, well, I'd say a few per cent of what it would cost on a properly settled world. Those kids are conditioned out of expecting anything better than what they get! Android staple is all they're given to eat and that's just an alga fortified with cheap additives; they're raised like the ancient red Indians not to be cold when they're naked in a temperate climate; and all the time their future employment is held up before them like a vision of paradise. If it hadn't been for Lars Talibrand's extraordinary birth—"

"What about it? What was so extraordinary?"

Horn explained, and Dize nodded very slowly several times. "Now that explains something I've never understood," he muttered. "Sometimes we've had androids aboard who'd already been in employment and lived in regular android barracks and so on—like for example learning a special trade before being passed on to Earth. That's another reason why I'd not have marked you out, of course, if you hadn't spoken up.

"There's a sort of mythology circulating among them. I guess they must know about Talibrand. Because these more experienced ones tell the others they may turn out to have been human-born, and if they work well and patiently and don't get into trouble, then maybe one day Talibrand will show up—at least, I guess that's who they mean, but I never heard his name mentioned. And when he does they'll be able to wash in some special liquid that takes away the blue and turn into regular human beings...."

He shrugged. "I always imagined it was some story a bright guy started simply to keep androids in line. Never paid it any mind."

"It fits," Horn said somberly. "I don't know about washing off the blue, because from what I can gather it's something that permeates the whole system and can't be got rid of once it's circulating. But the rest of it—*ach!* It makes me sick, you know? To think that Talibrand's work was actually being turned against him! They're clever devils to have exploited the news that way!"

There was a pause. At length Dize said, "Well, what are you going to do now—stick around and try to move those blockhead officials, hm?"

Horn shook his head.

"Well, I don't see you have much choice," Dize objected. "I mean, blued up like you are, even if I come along and swear to your identity, who's going to sell you passage to Creew 'n Dith? Androids aren't allowed to buy starflight ticket! And—and come to think of it, I guess you haven't any money or ID or ..." He spread both hands helplessly.

"Shembo," Horn said. "He'll recognize me, same as you did. All I need to do is hide for a while, see if I can avoid the same fate as Lars Talibrand. When I get to Creew 'n Dith, Braithwin will believe me okay."

"Hadn't thought of that," Dize admitted. "Okay, I'll get you home with me and go find out when Shembo's next due to land. Say, by the way!"

"Yes?"

"Did you find out who actually killed Talibrand?"

"No, and I don't care. Because I know it was his brother Jan who sold him out."

CHAPTER XVIII

MAJ-BRITH was astonished to see her husband returning so soon after she had seen him off to the port on another voyage to Earth, but the moment he had a chance to explain to her how Horn had been kidnapped and blued, she was fierce in her praise of what he had done—thinking, perhaps, of her own two boys currently out at school.

"All I've done so far," Horn corrected her dispiritedly, "is trip over things that were lying in front of me and fall with my nose in a pile of dirty facts! Right this very moment Captain Larrow is probably loading the androids I was with down at the port, and I don't stand a chance of preventing him. Here's this vast evil network spreading among the stars like the mycelium of a fungus, and I can't even chop off a few of its tendrils!"

"You haven't done so badly so far," Dize grunted. "You've cost them a key man on Earth—I mean, Coolin must have been pretty important, mustn't he? Someone infiltrated into the lawforce is bound to be useful whichever planet he's working on."

"But he can't have been the only one of his kind," Horn sighed. "I mean, it stretches belief that they should have been able to maneuver Talibrand to one particular hotel in one particular city where he was bound to run foul of Coolin. Poor devil! Talibrand, I mean. I only just thought how frustrating it must have been for him, knowing he was being pursued, to discover that of all times of the year he'd picked the eve of carnival week to arrive on Earth. Nothing gets done during carnival!"

"Stop blaming yourself for not being superhuman!" Dize rapped. "Coolin wasn't the only one—there were the two dealers right here on Newholme that you came close to exposing, and if only Kyer hadn't beaten a quick retreat we'd have had him, too. Here, have a drink and relax for a bit."

"I can see why Mr. Horn is so upset," Maj-Brith said, as she offered them a trayful of glasses. "I mean, the moment people were told that these alleged androids were actually enslaved human children, you'd expect them to be so—so *revolted* . . .!"

"I expected that myself," Horn admitted. "I must have been delirious, I guess. Because, you see, the key to this whole nasty business lies on Earth, not on any of the outworlds. I recall Braithwin telling me that when Lars Talibrand first proved to them that at least one child had been stolen away and disguised as an android they were so furious they came near to banning the trade from Creewndithian spaceports, but they were talked out of it by Jan Talibrand—for reasons which are now pretty obvious. I recall you yourself, Dize, telling me that androids are so expensive right here on Newholme that virtually no one owns any, and they all get shipped straight on to Earth. No, if even Lars Talibrand with the full authority of a citizen of the galaxy couldn't break a crucial link in the android trade-routes, that must be because it's not worth spending the energy. If Creew 'n Dith bans the trade, it goes via Vernier; if Vernier bans it, then they simply go to a longer way around, through Lygos maybe. Earth is the whole and sole support for the trade.

"And down there androids are so much a part of people's lives it's going to take a nova-sized outburst of publicity to break the habit of accepting them the same way one accepts robots!" He hesitated. "Know why I quit arguing with that fool of a lawforce commissioner?"

Dize shook his head.

"Something hit me all of a sudden, and I had to get out before it occurred to him, too. Look, here I am, the grandson of Earth's biggest producer of sophisticated

135

robots! How long is it going to be before the android traders start the rumor going to say, 'Ah! This means that Horn & Horn are all set to produce a new model robot competitive with androids and they're trying to scare people off!"

Dize's jaw dropped. "Hey! That's terrible—but you're quite right. I'd have fallen for an argument like that, and probably sweated like hell to keep the trade going. It's my livelihood, after all."

"Right. And it wouldn't make any difference that I can truthfully say I was more or less raised by an android. Our family's butler Rowl was a sort of extra parent to me, because my father's spent his whole life under grandad's shadow and takes out his resentment on my mother and . . . ah, skip it." He drew a deep breath. "But they weren't celebrating carnival together when I left, and it wasn't the first time that had happened."

"But there must be something you could do," Maj-Brith insisted doggedly. "Can't you—well, why not take people out to this place where you were taken, and let them see for themselves how the children are being processed?"

"How do I find my way? How do I tell which of a hundred suns it goes around? I saw maybe a couple of square miles of the surface—I can't even guess whether it's an uninhabited world or just some lonely corner of a colonized one."

"Well then . . ." Her determination was wilting. "Can't you tell the androids themselves the truth?"

"Wouldn't work. The deeper they became involved, the more the android traders must have covered themselves against the risk of their victims catching on. I thought for a while that the disappearance of female androids was due to accidents like the conception of Lars Talibrand; now I'm inclined to feel it was more of an extra precaution taken on general grounds. The process of human reproduction requires bisexuality. By not only conditioning the androids against sexual urge, but also

136

reducing them to wholly masculine company, they made the story of their artificial origin more credible on the subconscious level. Besides which, most androids don't *want* to think of themselves as human—at least, not until they've been long enough in work to relax and start thinking for themselves, like Dordy. Why should anyone want to be like the dealers and spacemen whose hands the androids pass through? All respect to you, Dize. But on the way here I was—ah—exposed to people who made Larrow and Shembo look like pure white angels!"

"I believe you," Dize muttered, staring down into his glass. "I've seen the condition of some of their cargoes when they got to Newholme—legs and arms broken, skin eruptions, bowel trouble. ..." He tossed back the remainder of his drink and rose.

"Well, I'll get along to the port, find out when Shembo's next due to stop over here. It's not likely to be more than a few days from now—he's been working the Newholme-Creew 'n Dith route regularly for several years."

"But be discreet," Horn warned. "If one word of my presence leaks out, there'll be all hell to pay."

It couldn't have been due to Dize talking too freely, nor to his sons—who were overjoyed to find their family involved in a "real adventure"—boasting among their school friends: Horn would have wagered his life on that. The boys were too sensible and Dize was too wary. So it must have been due to Kyer, who had managed to elude the lawforce.

A bomb was thrown at Dize's house two days later.

Miraculously, it fell into the channel of the heating conduits which drew down air from the front of the building to be conditioned in the basement. It exploded ten feet below the floor and spent its force on inanimate machinery; none of the occupants sustained worse than the cut across the head which Horn suffered because he was standing alongside one of the warm-air outlets and the blast knocked a picture down on him.

When the lawforce turned up to investigate, he kept well in the background, knowing what effect his blue skin was likely to have on their attitude towards him, and when Dize had finished talking to the visitors and came to report, he knew his caution had not been misplaced. The spaceman was fuming.

"We could have been killed!" he raged. "As it is, the house is a wreck—they'll have to dig out the whole ground floor before they can repair the heating! Blazes, I'm glad it's not midwinter with snow on the ground! I never had a serious brush with the lawforce before, but if this is how they act nowadays I'm surprised it's safe for a man to walk on a city street.!"

Horn shrugged. "I'm getting kind of tolerant about the failings of a modern lawforce. Really serious crimes are so rare on a world like Earth or Newholme they probably don't know the proper reactions. When I first came here I recall your being very proud of how quiet and comfortable this planet had become."

"Yes, but now I know what price we paid for our comfort!" Dize snorted. "Anyway, at least I have one good piece of news for you—Shembo makes his next planetfall tomorrow morning, and I've left a message for him to call here directly he's free."

It was an unusually quiet Shembo who listened to Horn's story, sipping meantime at the liquor Maj-Brith had poured for him.

"This make many strange things plain," he said at last.

"Such as what?" Horn leaned forward.

"Like ... well, you know biggest port on Creew 'n Dith, my home port, belong on land of Talibrand family. Much excitement there about where you gone to, Mr. Horn! Jan Talibrand say you insult him, abuse friendship, so he order you out. Not so many people believe, hm? But he a hereditary councillor and call him liar is kind of insulting to self, hm? Bad for all people of Creew 'n Dith! So then

138

ossip say this story you are asked for because you leave
ecret to go look for missing boy like Lars Talibrand did,
vant to cover tracks and distract people. I not believe
hat neither. Still, not knowing truth, what to do?

"Then just lately things happen, like every time
ndroids come in port Talibrand men come look at them.
ll my crew, all human spacecrew, have hands washed to
ee if they hide blue skin. All ships the same!" Shembo
rained his glass and beamed at Maj-Brith for offering
im a refill.

"All plain now. Talibrand looking for you. Looking
amn hard. Talibrand *scared!*"

"Good," said Horn unsympathetically. "But how the
evil am I going to make a landing on Creew 'n Dith if
`alibrand is keeping such a keen watch for me? I had
hought of putting some kind of cosmetic on to cover my
kin, but if he's alive to that notion ..." He shook his
ead, staring at the blue backs of his hands.

There was a pause. At length Horn said, "Look,
aptain Shembo, there's something I ... well, let me put it
his way. I really do appreciate your helping me, but if I
ucceed in what I'm trying to do, won't that mean that
've taken away your livelihood?"

Shembo shrugged. "This bad, androids turn out to be
uman kids. This make me sick to stomach. I not go on
vith any more than I help, hm? I got contract to fill, and I
uess it take weeks, months maybe, before news comes
ight down *here*." He laid his hand on his belly. "But is not
oing to take away my living, Mr. Horn! I'm spaceman,
arry whatever people say I ought. Is been long time since
utworlds so poor they only can sell to Earth androids. Is
ow factories, is people with real natural animal hides,
urs, spices, all kinds of luxury things from primitive
vorlds which Earth too clean and tidy to have. Maybe not
o good pay as androids, but still good things to make
rade."

"What he says is quite true," Dize confirmed. "These
ast few days I've been wondering what would become of

me if the android-robot trade dried up, and I reached pretty much the same conclusion. In fact, I told Maj Brith last night I thought it might be sensible if I started looking out for a master's post now instead of waiting til Larrow retires. I could be one of the people who got into the new kind of trade ahead of the rush."

"You do that," Maj-Brith said firmly. "I don't want you to make a single trip more with androids aboard."

"That's a load off my mind," Horn murmured. "And what's more, that would bring real benefits to the outworlds, too. Instead of just collecting a commission on the transshipment of android cargoes, they could offer their own products ... Although frankly right now couldn't care less if the withdrawal of the android brought the whole structure of galactic trade crashing down on our heads. It might even be good for us—teach u a lesson we wouldn't forget in a hurry!"

There was renewed silence. At length he became aware that Shembo was nodding his head slowly back and forth "I have idea," said the Creewndithian. "I guess maybe know how we get you safe to Braithwin."

The key to Shembo's plan was the timing of thei planetfall. The ship dropped through the night toward the spaceport on the Talibrand estate an hour and a hal before local dawn, in the dead part of the night when men's minds are sluggish and their bodies weary—th part of the night, too, when Jan Talibrand was least likel to come out as he occasionally did and personall supervise the inspection of incoming spacecrew.

He was not only worried about android cargoes Shembo said, although clearly the best and mos anonymous way for Horn to make his return to Creew 'n Dith was hidden among a group of androids; that however, would have implied arranging transit ou beyond Creew 'n Dith and transfer there to a vessel boun inwards towards Earth. Consequently any strange arriving on the planet was instantly suspected.

Horn smiled grimly at the information. Even if h

140

wasn't called to account for his crimes, it sounded as though Jan Talibrand was likely to go the same way as his father Barg and die insane.

Which would be a very appropriate fate for him.

The ship touched down, and port guards—roused from sleep and grumbling to each other—came out to put the crew through the newly instituted checks and searches and to probe the crated robots that composed the majority of the cargo with portable sonic projectors in case there was a man hidden among them.

Between the inner and outer doors of one of the cargo locks, Horn waited tensely as the inspectors approached. They were almost upon him when what he had been expecting took place, and a commotion broke out on the far side of the ship. Voices yelled orders in Creewndithian; lights sprang up and swept that part of the field. The guards who had been so close to Horn hurried to see what the trouble was, drawing guns as they ran. The moment they were out of the way, Horn dropped to the ground and ran for dear life.

By the time they discovered one of Shembo's crewmen, acting drunk and laughing his head off at the success of the "practical joke" he had played on the guards, Horn was safely concealed among two high stacks of stored goods near the exit from the port.

Having been caught out once and made to look fools, the guards would be wary of a second such trick—so Shembo had argued. They would disregard suspicious noises in case they proved to be bait for a further trap.

It looked as though he was perfectly correct. Horn was close enough to hear what went on as the guards dragged the crewman to the port authority building, and later as he was sent back in Shembo's personal care to the ship, the captain slanging him unmercifully to deceive his listeners. After that, things quieted down. They would wait, Shembo had predicted, until after dawn to start unloading the cargo.

When all was still, he crept warily to the gate, found the

man there snoozing, and stole past him more silently than a shadow. A hundred yards beyond, he broke into a run, and the first flush of red on the eastern sky found him hammering at the door of Braithwin's hall, infinitely thankful not to have lost his way and been isolated on the streets when enough folk were about for his blue skin to become conspicuous.

Unlike Jan Talibrand, Braithwin did not feel the need to surround himself with retainers and guards. It took a good five minutes' battering with both fists to provoke the appearance of a sleepy-eyed porter, who on seeing—as he assumed—an android knocking, snarled an insult and made to close again.

"Take me to Hereditary Councillor Braithwin!" ordered Horn. "Bring him from bed if he's still asleep!"

"Fool!" the porter countered. "Today is a session of the Hereditary Council, and he was up late last night planning the business it's to deal with!"

"So much the better! Go tell him I have a message from Lars Talibrand, a message from the dead. And he will listen."

Invoking the name of one who, since his death, was publicly known to have been a citizen of the galaxy secured the porter's grudging consent. It was almost comical to see the change of expression on his face when he returned.

"Come inside!" he said, swallowing hard. "Councillor Braithwin will indeed receive you, and prays you to wait in the great hall until he comes!"

And in the hall, puffy with sleep and still belting his undress robe around him, Braithwin shouted with amazement to see Horn, whom he confessed to have believed long dead. He stood there, and listened, and lastly gave a grim nod.

"Today the Hereditary Council meets," he said. "We have come from all over Creew 'n Dith to plan the coming year. But first we shall sit in judgement!"

CHAPTER XIX

THERE WERE twenty of the hereditary councillors, all men: two very old, two whose youth suggested they must lately have assumed posts formerly held by aged predecessors, the rest of Braithwin's age give or take a few years. A table had been set up for them in the great hall, with pens and paper and a neat sheaf of printed reports before each chair. An hour and a half after dawn they began to assemble. Those who came from close at hand arrived yawning and stretching, some having traveled by groundcar through the night; those who had come from further away had slept last night as guests of Braithwin, and greeted the new day fresh and rested.

He saluted each as they joined him in the hall and went to warm themselves at one of the open fires or selected breakfast from trays held by attentive girls. A barrel of the sour Creewndithian beer stood waiting to be tapped later.

Of them all, Jan Talibrand arrived last, when Braithwin had already taken his place at the head of the table. The showy recent-model Earth-built groundcar hummed to a halt outside, and the carefully dressed, impeccably barbered, fragrantly scented occupant made his entry with a flourish. Only dark rings below his eyes betrayed the fact that he had spent the past weeks in mortal terror of exposure.

He took his place at the table, acknowledged greetings from his colleagues, and turned expectantly towards Braithwin. Their eyes met for an instant; then Braithwin looked down at the papers before him.

"This day are we the hereditary councillors of this planet met together that we shall hear how it goes with our people, their business and their livings, how justice rules, how prosperity increases, how there is peace abroad on Creew 'n Dith, and where business fails, life passes, justice is found wanting, prosperity wanes or peace gives place to war, to set speedily about righting the same. I am Braithwin of Braithwin; I am here and undertake faithfully to discharge the tasks of a member of this council."

He touched the man on his left, and the sequence of declarations went in turn around the table according to ancient custom. His eyes followed the words, but seemed to linger longest on one face in particular.

"I am Talibrand of Talibrand; I am here and undertake faithfully to discharge the tasks of a member of this council."

Was there a certain insolence in that tone? Braithwin dragged his gaze away.

He shuffled the papers before him, feeling his heart pound as he lifted the first of them, the one which none of the other councillors had been given. He licked his lips.

"I hereby declare this council open and do impeach one of our number namely Jan Talibrand of the house of Talibrand and maintain that he sits among us not by right but by arrogant presumption for that he has crimes unanswered for—"

The rest began to understand at that point what was being said, and were turning to stare at him in astonishment. Talibrand himself had not moved a muscle, but he had gone completely white.

Up to now Braithwin had been almost droning his words, for the opening of the council was a standard ritual. Now he adopted a fiercer tone and gave the words their individual stress.

"In that: First, he has conspired with others being or not being citizens of this planet to steal away and sell into slavery divers human beings, particularly children, and to profit thereby, the said action being contrary to law and natural justice.

144

"Second, he conspired with others being or not being citizens of this planet to contrive the death by violence of his brother Lars Talibrand of the house of Talibrand, a citizen of the galaxy.

"Third, he of his personal responsibility did steal away and sell into slavery one Derry Horn, a citizen of the planet Earth."

Braithwin had to lick his lips again as he returned the paper to the pile.

"Jan Talibrand, what answer give you to these charges?"

The eyes of all the councillors turned to fix on Talibrand, but he paid them no heed. He was slowly rising to his feet, staring at the door to Braithwin's sanctum. The rest of the company followed his gaze and there saw emerging . . .

An android. A blue-skinned man with a full black beard, dark piercing eyes, who lifted his right arm and pointed at Talibrand like a witch-smeller passing sentence of death!

Talibrand's nerve broke in that instant; he uttered a sound like a sob and fled headlong from the hall.

"Stop him!" Braithwin cried, but he was too late. Before anyone could reach the door in pursuit, the waiting groundcar had hummed swiftly away.

"Perhaps it's as well," Braithwin rumbled, calming the other members of the council. "I would not have any man on my beloved planet held guilty on no better judgement than that of his own blind terror! Sit you down again, my friends, and hear out what I have to say before you act. Likely he will make for his estate, and we'll follow him there later if you agree that the charges you have heard require an answer. Now here!"—he gestured at Horn, waiting beside his presidential chair.

"Here is an android, or so you will have believed. But for all the blueness of his skin, this is a man—that Derry Horn of whom you've doubtless heard."

A rustle of amazement passed through the company,

and the councillors resumed their seats.

"He speaks only a snatch of Creewndithian, but we speak, I believe, at least a little Anglic among us. I will ask him to tell you his reasons for maintaining that there has *never* been a genuine android on Creew 'n Dith, but only such disguised human victims as himself. If that is your wish . . .?"

The oldest member of the council, who had been too stiff to stir his aged bones in the general rush after Talibrand, coughed and moved that the testimony should be heard. At a gesture from Braithwin, Horn—who had been able to follow what was going on since so much of it spoke for itself—sawed, planed, nailed together the coffin which would bury Jan Talibrand.

In full formal array the Hereditary Council of Creew 'n Dith arrived before the gates of the Talibrand estate to demand an answer to the charges made against its owner, and found the way barred. Sensing Horn's impatience, Braithwin had warned him beforehand that if this proved to be the case they would merely set guards around the boundary and close the spaceport, leaving any thought of a formal trial until after they had disposed of regular business; as he had rightly pointed out, the welfare of a whole planetary population must take precedence over a single criminal, no matter how heinous his acts might have been, and the council had many demands on its time.

And that was what would probably have happened but for the sudden advent of a gunshot, fired, perhaps, by some nervous and over-loyal retainer. Doubtless it had been aimed at Horn, whose blue skin marked him out as a conspicuous target among the councillors and their attendants, but it missed by so narrow a margin that it scorched the skin of his cheek, and found the withered chest of the oldest member of the council, who had remained behind in his groundcar.

That settled the matter. The wanton slaughter of a

member of the hereditary council was an insult to the entire planet of Crew 'n Dith, and no one could rest easy until the affront was avenged. As though realizing he was doomed, Talibrand unleashed full-scale fire on the party, and with spent shot tapping at the roofs of their cars they retired to assemble their retainers and lay formal siege to the Talibrand estate.

They moved in at nightfall, breaking the boundary fence at two or three places and sending a detachment up through the spaceport to provide a distraction for the defences. Braithwin politely but firmly advised Horn to stay in the background.

"For one thing," the councillor pointed out, "even though it's dark your blue skin will make you a prime target—and your evidence is our chief weapon against Talibrand, so I don't dare lose you. For another, this has turned into a private affair. What mainly counts right now is not just that Talibrand has engaged in an evil trade, or even that he's contrived the murder of the brother we so much admired. It's simply that he's brought shame on the hereditary council of Crew 'n Dith, and it's for us to wipe out that shame!"

Nodding his comprehension, Horn dutifully drew aside.

In the wood which fringed the estate, twigs broke and their tiny reports were followed by others, louder, and sometimes by a scream. Across open fields dark shadows moved, and here and there knives flashed and grunting struggles ended in bloody gurgling sounds. But the approach was slow; the Talibrand estate had been laid out in days when sieges like these were not uncommon, and it was well to be able to defend the land against a greedy intruder. That was the advantage the defenders enjoyed. Set against it was the fact that many of the attackers had been guests of the Talibrands, particularly in the old days when Barg was head of the house, and they knew all the weak spots in the perimeter.

By the time the night had ebbed away, the defenders had been forced to close in on the hall. But having accomplished that much, having cleansed the outlying grounds of all but a handful of Talibrand's retainers who might snipe at and harass his own men, Braithwin sighed and ordered general retrenchment.

"I know that hall, and it's the next best thing to a fortress," he mused for the benefit of any of his companions who might choose to listen. "It won't fall except to bombs or starvation. And since we'd rather have Talibrand alive . . .Hell! Horn, what are you doing here! I told you to keep out of this!"

Emerging from the cover of the bush he had used to screen his approach, Horn shrugged.

"It sounded quieter, so I decided to come and see what was happening. I told someone on Newholme I was going to take Talibrand apart with my bare hands, but since I can't hold myself to the promise I thought at least I deserve a sight of the finish."

"Finish!" Braithwin snorted. "You'll have to wait a long time for that!" He gestured towards the long low rambling hall, dimly outlined against the greying sky of dawn. "That's one of the oldest Creewndithian manor houses, you know! When that was built, people took it for granted they might have to sweat out a seven-month winter on what supplies they'd managed to store! I could just bring it crashing about Talibrand's ears, but I'd hate to do that, frankly. I'd risk killing retainers of his whose only crime is that they adhered to the Creewndithian faith, and stayed loyal. *I* know the Talibrand clan! There's not one in fifty of them Jan Talibrand would dare enlist in his filthy game!"

"Well, if some of his retainers would rather not be involved, couldn't you—?"

"Buy them off, turn them into traitors?" Braithwin scowled like a thundercloud. "I said it and I mean it: Creewndithians are loyal! And I wouldn't have it any other way!"

Feeling as though he had unwittingly insulted the older man, Horn turned away and stared through the morning twilight towards the lowering bulk of the Talibrand hall. Occasionally a shot spurted from the embrasure of a window, marking the huge mass with a speck of brightness, but otherwise there was no sign of life up there.

And yet, at one end of the rambling structure, surely one of the granaries or storehouses or whatever they were was growing larger . . . ?

"Braithwin!" he cried. "You were wrong! There's smoke rising—someone's set the place on fire!"

In the same moment, the first tongues of flame smeared upward across the smoke.

"Who the . . . ?" Braithwin planted his feet four-square on Talibrand ground and slapped the hilt of his sword with his palm. "Never mind, never mind! Whoever it was has done us a service. They won't survive long in there without burning or suffocating! To me Braithwin—hey, hey, to me, to me!"

He departed at a run, leaving Horn to stare thoughtfully as the flames mounted even higher above the house.

Whoever was responsible, the fire was doing its work. Soon sparks were belching from windows on the lower floors as the rising morning wind carried it along interconnecting passages designed to maintain the house's integrity under seige. The shots from snipers' guns had formerly cracked forth at all points of the building; within ten minutes of the outbreak they were confined to the end furthest from the conflagration.

How long could the occupants endure this? Horn clenched his fingers so hard the nails bit deep into his palms. The wind was turning the whole structure into a horizontal chimney now, with smoke leaking from half a hundred places far from the original blaze. The roof of the section where the flames had first appeared caved in suddenly, and the underbelly of the smoke-pall was lit with ruddy flashes. Making the most of the distraction, Braithwin was marshaling his forces for an advance on the house.

The first chip of the sun showed above the eastern skyline, and a moment later the great main doors were thrown open. A smoke-grimed woman in a ragged gown, coughing and choking, ran out waving a streamer of white cloth on the end of a pole, and behind her emerged a straggling line of girls and young children, not a few of them howling with terror. The attackers parted ranks to let them seek safety in the fields and woods.

Shivering a little—the house of Talibrand had been a beacon-light throughout the history of Crew 'n Dith, and to execute justice on its current overlord was a task little to his liking—Braithwin heard the cries and thought: a *funeral dirge fit for a fratricide!*

The spot at which he had lately encountered Horn was among the best vantage points to survey the house from; having disposed his forces to meet all eventualities, he returned to it, and was puzzled not to find Horn still nearby. Where had the fool gone now? Did he not realize he was the person on whom all the evidence against Talibrand—

"Stand to! Stand to!"

The sergeants' shouts ran down the line of men like the wave made in a field of standing corn by the passage of a gust of wind. All else forgotten, Braithwin realized that following the departure of the women and children Talibrand had not ordered the doors of his great hall to be closed again, and that meant he must be intending a sally, to sell his life dearly. And here they came!

Within seconds the sally became a melee as the besiegers broke from cover and met the charge of the defenders head on. The range was too close for most of the available guns; this was bladework, and it was hard to tell which swords were red with blood, which with the glare of the fire. Only the screams of the dying indexed the progress of the fight, and screams were neutral, after all....

At first Braithwin merely stood by, reflecting sourly that Talibrand's men didn't stand a chance. All it would take to decide the outcome of this was time. With nineteen families ranged against one, the result was foregone, which must be why Jan Talibrand had resolved to cut short—

Braithwin's thought slewed away at right angles, and he gazed wildly about him. Only a moment ago Horn had told of his own resolution, to deal personally with Talibrand, and now his prey was out in the open he had his chance.

"The fool!" Braithwin exclaimed. "If he's risking his neck I'll have him flayed, I'll . . .! Oh, the *fool!*"

He dragged his sword from its sheath and headed incontinently for the spot at which, as was obvious from the dense cluster of Talibrand's retainers all around it, Jan Talibrand had decided to make his stand, on the lawn before the wide main doors.

"Horn!" Braithwin shouted. "Have you seen Horn?" And, as though inadvertently, when he discovered he was addressing a Talibrand man, his sword parted head from neck. "Horn! The blue man—have you seen him?" Once more, a Talibrand man, and the sword clicked and jiggled against another like it and sank deep into yielding muscle. "Horn! I'm looking for—"

Talibrand.

In pure astonishment Braithwin realized that the last man he had cut down had fallen to reveal the long face, the long limbs and the long sword dripping gore of the fratricide Jan Talibrand himself. All else was on the instant forgotten. His mind filling with fury, he leapt forward shouting a cry he had had from his father's father's father and never thought to use in actual conflict.

"A Braithwin! A *Bra-a-ai-thwi-i-i-in!*"

And on the final beat of the rhythmical shout he knocked aside one of his own retainers to leave a clear field of sweep for the blade that cut through Talibrand's sword-arm and through his rib cage and through his shoulder blade and his spine and last of all through his foul black heart.

Disbelieving, Braithwin stared at what he had done, letting go his hilt and watching it describe a curious irregular curve as Talibrand's weight bore it to the ground. Retainers crowded around, plying him with congratulations, but he remembered why he had come here originally and barked harsh questions.

"Horn! Where is he? Have you seen him?"

None of them knew.

CHAPTER XX

THE HOUSE was blazing fiercely now, its long timber-strutted roof flaming along half its total length, and smoke was welling even from the double doors of the great hall which had been furthest from the fire. By the light of the flames Braithwin set off on a round of the area, demanding of everyone he met what could have happened to Horn. He had made nearly the full circuit of the house before anyone gave him a positive answer: a boy holding one hand to his brow to prevent blood from a cut scalp running into his eyes.

"Why, yes, I did see the blue man—there near the door of the great hall a while ago! And, Councillor, is it true that you personally—?"

But Braithwin was gone, furiously.

Back at his starting-point, he folded his arms on his chest and scowled. Well, that seemed pretty conclusive! If he had indeed been up here, and yet only one person had had a chance to see and remember him, that meant he hadn't lasted very long. Small wonder. Granted he was a cut or two above the average Earthman, he still oughtn't to have matched himself with men of Crew 'n Dith. Probably when the funeral parties were clearing up they'd run across his blue body, unique among the rest of the dead, and—

A shout went up among those around him, and hands pointed towards the house. Braithwin whirled. From the smoke-belching double doorway, a dark figure was staggering with a limp white burden in his arms. Men rushed from every side to help, for he was half suffocating with the smoke and his eyes were almost blinded by tears.

"Careful there!" he croaked as he gave up the girl he had brought out. "She's the wife of a very great man. . . ."

"Councillor Braithwin had already informed me," Horn explained in husky tones, "that no retainer on Creew 'n Dith would turn against his master in time of trouble. So it could hardly have been one of the staff who set the fire. That left one likely candidate among those inside the house."

"Moda Talibrand," Braithwin grunted.

"Right. I knew she hated her brother-in-law—and with good reason, of course, though she only had her suspicions to go by. So I went down and made some inquiries of the women and children who'd been given safe-conduct from the house. She wasn't there. And when someone realized she'd been with them when they assembled to make their dash for safety in the great hall, and wasn't among them now, there was only one possible conclusion: Jan Talibrand had kept her back to burn alive in the fire she herself had started. And there she was, lying where Talibrand had thrown her under a serving-table. So I brought her out."

He raised his beer-mug and poured the contents down his throat. He was acquiring the taste for the stuff, he decided, and held the mug out for more.

Around the table in Braithwin's great hall, the surviving councillors nodded approval. They had rested after the battle, and before resuming their interrupted business they were refreshing themselves with food and drink.

"At the risk of pre-empting the official verdict," Braithwin commented gruffly. "I can't help feeling the planet is a better place without someone who could revenge himself that way upon a helpless woman ... hrr'hm!"

Clearing his throat, he noisily rustled his stack of papers together.

"For the benefit of our distinguished visitor Derry Horn, I propose to transact a small part of our next business in Anglic. First: a motion. It is resolved that no more so-called 'androids' be permitted passage through Creewndithian ports, and henceforth it shall be an offense for any Creewndithian citizen to engage in traffic in them. Aye?"

Every hand was raised.

"Second: a motion. It is resolved that Derry Horn, a citizen of the planet Earth, be granted the honorary citizenship of Creew 'n Dith. Aye?"

Again, every hand went up.

"Third: an entry of record. Jan Talibrand of the house of Talibrand formerly of this council did for causes by this council in their several persons witnessed forfeit his right and the right of his descendants to the rank of hereditary councillor. Aye?"

And a third time agreement.

"Good," said Braithwin, and sat back. "Well, there's no need to detain you further, Mr. Horn—you'll hardly be interested even with your new honorary status as a Creewndithian citizen in the rather elaborate procedure of nominating Talibrand's successor ... anyhow, it's not legal for anyone but councillors to be present! I'll arrange for your citizenship papers to be prepared at once, and once you have them you can depart for Earth whenever you wish. Though there is, of course, one other small problem we've been considering—the fact that your skin is at present blue."

Horn shrugged. "People are going to have to get used, even on Earth, to the fact that blue skins don't label

154

rtificial men that can be treated as simple property."

"Yes, but even so I think you'd be the first to grant that getting rid of the dye would help the process of adjustment. Now it's been suggested, and we agree, that as a—hah!—a near-friend of a citizen of the galaxy you might find another of that distinguished company willing to assist you. I've already sent a message to Gayk on Vernier, offering what funds may be required to develop an antidote to the android blue."

He fumbled in his belt-pouch. "And, speaking of citizens of the galaxy ... ah, here we are." He withdrew the grey wallet that had formerly belonged to Lars Talibrand. "I think there is no one in whose hands we could more aptly leave this relic which was discovered in the ashes of Talibrand Hall?" He made it a question, and the councillors answered with vigorous nods.

Accepting the certificate, Horn rose. He had intended to speak, to utter formal thanks, but he was too overcome to do more than bow his head and turn towards the door of Braithwin's study. He had left the hall, and closed the door of the small room behind them, before he realized that the other person present, whom from the corner of his eye he had taken for a mere serving-wench, was Moda Talibrand.

She had put off her mourning garb and resumed the plain white Creewndithian gown. Her face was full of a strange mixture of sorrow and happiness.

There was a long silence. When at last she spoke, it was in a tone which suggested she was resuming a conversation that had been briefly interrupted.

"You know, I have two reasons for being glad that Lars's work has been completed after all. The first is obvious—that anything he so prized as to risk his life was worth doing and I couldn't help but want to see it done, too. But the second reason is hardly clear even to me. Perhaps I can put it like this.

"I thought there could only be one man like my Lars in the whole galaxy, and once I'd lost him I could have no

155

further reason for wanting to live. But I was wrong. There are other men like him. I've met one of them, and where there are two there must be many, many more."

She reached out impulsively and seized his hand. He bowed his head. A lump rose in his throat. He was thinking of a red-haired man lying dead with a knife in his chest on the floor of a room on Earth.

The word went out. . . .

They told Shembo that no more androids would be shipped through Creew 'n Dith, and that his livelihood was gone. He beamed with a flash of teeth and refrained from mentioning that his next inbound cargo was already on order: furs, cured hides, and rough-cut natural gemstones too random for machines to duplicate.

All he said was, "Must be trade!"

They told Dize the same, and he brushed the information aside; he was too busy studying up for the examination which would make him master of his own ship instead of a junior officer to Larrow. It had amused his sons greatly to find their father going back to school.

Also the word came to a place where battered ancient starships put down on a hard salt-pan beside a sluggish sea, and the wind seemed to turn chillier with its coming. But on Arthworld, and Vernier, and Lygos, and many others where for decades no mother had known when she might have to weep for the loss of a child stolen by kidnappers, it was more as if the sun had broken through a cloud.

It came to Earth, and Derry Horn senior spoke frowningly to his father, saying, "That whippersnapper of a son of mine seems to have kicked up quite a ruckus out yonder!"

"Wrecked our export balances, for one thing!" Grandfather Horn grunted, studying reports which said that Arthworld and Venier had followed the lead of Creew 'n Dith in banning the android trade, and that Lygos was expected to join them shortly.

156

Then both together lifted their eyes worriedly to look at the butler, Rowl, and wondered: *does he know?*

The word traveled fastest of all, of course, among the androids; it had already passed along the trade routes before the ban began to interfere with the traffic.

Androids were used to conversing through a third party; in one such conversation which followed the arrival of the news on Earth the intermediary was the driver of a garbage wagon that served the hotel where Lars Talibrand had died, who bunked in the same android barracks as Berl of the wreck-salvage squad.

From Berl to Dordy the driver carried the opening remarks: "What do you know? *I* never thought that soft-looking boy would make out! Say, what are you going to do when they get the message down here and have to repeal the regulations that keep us on the hook? First off, *I'm* going to—"

There followed a list of wild fantasies, most of which would have called for androids to be freed from the laws of nature as well as the laws of man to make them possible. When they were relayed to Dordy he smiled, and sent back his answer crisp, concise and as the fruit of much quiet thought.

"Start a campaign to have Derry Horn made a citizen of the galaxy!"

THE END

DRAGONDRUMS
   by ANNE McCAFFREY

Piemur, a boy soprano, had been chosen out of all the singers at the Harperhall of Pern for the leading role in the dramatic choral work to be presented at Lord Groghe's Gather. But during practice one day his voice broke – and suddenly his whole future at the Harperhall seemed uncertain.

But Masterharper Robinton, Menolly and Sebell had other plans for Piemur – they were sure that his quick wits and discretion could be used to keep a check on the troublesome Oldtimers and their strange traffic in fire lizards.

So whilst serving as a messenger-drum apprentice, Piemur carried out special errands for the three. And it was on one such errand that he realized his wildest dream – and got into deeper trouble than ever before . . .

0 552 11804 4 – £1.25

DRAGONSONG
by ANNE McCAFFREY

Menolly-Mistress of Music, Ward of Fire Lizards

Every two hundred years or so, shimmering threads fall, raining black ruin on Pern. The great dragons of Pern hurl themselves through the beleaguered skies, flaming tongues of fire to destroy deadly Thread and save the Planet. It was not Threadfall that made Menolly unhappy. It was her father who betrayed her ambition to be a Harper, who thwarted her love of music. Menolly had no choice but to run away. She came upon a group of fire lizards, wild relatives of the fire-breathing dragons. Her music swirled about them; she taught nine to sing. . . . Suddenly Mellony was no longer alone.

0 552 10661 5 – £1.25

DRAGONSINGER: HARPER OF PERN
by ANNE McCAFFREY

When Menolly, daughter of Yanas Sea Holder, arrived at the Harper Craft Hall, she came in style, aboard a bronze dragon followed by her nine fire lizards. The Masterharper of Pern aware of her unique skills, had chosen her as his only girl apprentice. But the holdness girl had first to overcome many heartaches in this strange new life. Two things sustained her; her devoted lizards – a subject on which she was fitted to instruct her Masters – and the music .. music of transcendent beauty, music-making where at last she was accepted. In the great Hall, Menolly could fulfill her destiny.

552 10881 2 – £1.50

A SELECTED LIST OF SCIENCE FICTION AND FANTASY IN CORGI

The prices shown below were correct at the time of going to press.

While every effort is made to keep prices low, it is sometimes necessary to increase prices at short notice. Corgi Books reserve the right to show new retail prices on covers which may differ from those previously advertised in the text or elsewhere.

The prices shown below were correct at the time of going to press.

☐	11669 6	**THE DRAGON LENSMAN**	*David Kyle*	£1.25
☐	11151 1	**FANTASTIC VOYAGE**	*Isaac Asimov*	85p
☐	13869 3	**STAR TREK 1**	*James Blish*	95p
☐	10746 8	**THE CABAL**	*Saul Dunn*	75p
☐	10886 3	**THE CABAL 2: THE BLACK MOON**	*Saul Dunn*	85p
☐	10694 1	**RAVEN: SWORDMISTRESS OF CHAOS**	*Richard Kirk*	70p
☐	10861 8	**RAVEN 2: A TIME OF GHOSTS**	*Richard Kirk*	80p
☐	11131 7	**RAVEN 5: A TIME OF DYING**	*Richard Kirk*	95p
☐	11313 1	**THE WHITE DRAGON**	*Anne McCaffrey*	£1.95
☐	10965 7	**GET OFF THE UNICORN**	*Anne McCaffrey*	£1.75
☐	10881 2	**DRAGONSINGER: HARPER OF PERN**	*Anne McCaffrey*	£1.50
☐	10661 5	**DRAGONSONG**	*Anne McCaffrey*	£1.25
☐	10773 5	**DRAGONFLIGHT**	*Anne McCaffrey*	£1.25
☐	11789 7	**DECISION AT DOONA**	*Anne McCaffrey*	£1.50
☐	11219 4	**THE CITY AND THE STARS**	*Arthur C. Clarke*	95p
☐	01077 8	**DRAGONWORLD**	*Byron Preiss &*	£3.95
			J. Michael Reaves	
☐	11178 3	**A CANTICLE FOR LEIBOWITZ**	*Walter M. Miller*	£1.25
☐	11194 5	**EARTH ABIDES**	*George R. Stewart*	£1.00

All these books are available at your bookshop or newsagent, or can be ordered direct from the publisher. Just tick the titles you want and fill in the form below.

CORGI BOOKS, Cash Sales Department, P.O. Box 11, Falmouth, Cornwall.

Please send cheque or postal order, no currency.

Please allow cost of book(s) plus the following for postage and packing:

U.K. Customers – Allow 45p for the first book, 20p for the second book and 14p for each additional book ordered, to a maximum charge of £1.63.

B.F.P.O. and Eire – Allow 45p for the first book, 20p for the second book plus 14p per copy for the next 7 books, thereafter 8p per book.

Overseas Customers – Allow 75p for the first book and 21p per copy for each additional book.

NAME (Block Letters) ....

ADDRESS ....

(June '82) ....